# CONEY ISLAND
# WONDER STORIES

## TALES OF THE CITY OF FIRE

# CONEY ISLAND WONDER STORIES

## TALES OF THE CITY OF FIRE

*edited by*
*Robert J. Howe & John Ordover*

WILDSIDE PRESS

DREAMLAND PRODUCTIONS

Wildside Press
www.wildsidepress.com

A Dreamland Productions book.

Design by Lee Willett/Studio 23
Cover photographs by William Howe

First edition: 2005
ISBN: 1-55742-349-0
Printed in the United States.

# Coney Island Wonder Stories

IN ALMOST EVERYONE'S CHILDHOOD there is some magical spot; some nexus where the everyday world touches another universe. Coney Island was that place in my own boyhood. In the late 1960s and early 1970s, the historical Coney Island was more apparent than it is today, in the decrepit shells of public baths, hotel facades camouflaged in graffiti, and the picked-apart skeletons of amusement park rides slowly rusting into the urban brownfields upon which they stood.

Coney Island was also the frontier. More than just a tacky collection of greasy boardwalk stands and souvenir shops, the wide sandy beach marked the end of North America. To stand on the sand and look seaward was to gaze on wonder.

Summers my mother would take us, my brother and me, on the F-train from Jay Street in downtown Brooklyn, to West 8th Street in Brighton Beach, the eastern half of Coney Island. The straight-line distance between our home in North Brooklyn and the Boardwalk wasn't more than seven miles, but in my imagination it was another continent. I used to think that the smell of creosote cooking out of the track ties on the elevated subway platforms was the smell of the sea.

Riding from North Brooklyn to Coney Island was like riding out to the country. The subway emerged briefly from the tunnel at Smith and Ninth streets—the first look at daylight and a peek at the Gowanus Canal; a toxic, greenish body of water that separates Red Hook from the rest of Brooklyn. The trains then had wooden overhead fans and wicker seats, and bits of straw scratched my legs.

At Ditmas Avenue the train would emerge into the sunshine again, and for the remainder of the ride south I'd stand at the front of the front car, next to the motorman in his tiny compartment, counting the stations and waiting for my first glimpse of the ocean.

The elevated stop at West Eighth Street was completely roofed over and had walls of corrugated steel—kind of a giant, elevated Quonset hut. At that time there was a connecting walkway to the New York Aquarium, usually our first stop on any trip to Coney Island. I'd bolt out the door of the train and into the salty breeze.

The magic began at the aquarium. Rather than seeing fish tanks, I was looking though windows into another world, scenes into which I could fall, trancelike, for long minutes at a time. As far back as I can remember, I was hypnotized by the sight of the ocean. I spent hours on end at the margin of sea and sand, staring out at the uncluttered horizon—the first place a city kid ever had an unobstructed view of the world. I would stand with my feet in the surf, imagining what it would be like to walk across the bottom of the ocean; seeing everything through the characteristic green tint of the Atlantic.

Bound up with the visual magic was the sensual. The taste of Nathan's Famous hot dogs, cotton candy, jelly apples and hot buttered corn. The smell of hot knishes, stale beer, greasy French fries, suntan lotion (this was the Coppertone era—decades before the word sunscreen meant anything), and the ocean. The springy resilience of the boardwalk and the salt breeze against sunburned cheeks; the fine grit of sand underfoot, on your corn on the cob, and in your bathing suit.

There was the wooden clatter of two roller coasters, the Cyclone (still operating) and the Thunderbolt (defunct, then partially destroyed by fire, and finally razed to make way for a minor-league ballpark), the shrieks of customers having a good time being terrified, the cries of the hawkers at a hundred crooked games of skill—everything from sharpshooting with BB rifles to ring tosses—and beneath it all, the susurrus of the surf and the barely perceptible hiss of sand moving in the breeze.

The real magic of Coney Island, though, the enchantment that transcends the manmade spectacle, is the magic of the frontier. Coney Island would never have had the visceral grab it exerts to this day if it were located in the middle of Kansas. As it is, perched on the aged edge of the continent, it is the gateway to our dreams.

The stories in this anthology, chosen by John Ordover and myself, capture some of the magic of the place. These tales are also frontiers, where the universe within rubs against the outside world. We stand always on the edge of wonder, I think, and need only to be pointed in the right direction to see it.

*Robert J. Howe*, June 2005

# Rose in Dreamland

*Kristine Kathryn Rusch*

ROSE FIRST WALTZED to "Dreamland" in 1910, at the age of nineteen, full skirts flowing, wisps of light brown hair curling about her face. She was tall as a man, slender, and prettier than any other woman in Fond du Lac County, prettier, maybe, than any other woman in Wisconsin. She danced at barn raisings, and fiddle festivals, at family gatherings and Sunday afternoon socials, man after man clasping her cinched waist. Matrons called her wanton, while secretly wishing they had moved as gracefully at so young an age. Men just watched and hoped that Rose would dance forever.

At twenty-one, she married, and hung up her dancing shoes. For her thirty-second birthday, her husband Henrich gave her a phonograph and a recording of a man she had never heard of singing "Dreamland." Henrich waltzed her around the living room, to the astonishment of their young son, who had never seen his parents dance, hug or even hold hands.

And all the while she thought of Dreamland.

· · ·

The prickly heat stuck to her face. Rose lifted her long skirts with one hand, held the heavy basket with the other, and walked across the sunbaked roadway. Amusement parks appeared around her, but she only had eyes for Dreamland, its white towers rising like a fairy city against the sky. Her body ached, and she could barely stand upright. People jostled her. Screams, cries and laughter echoed above the roar of the surf. She wanted to be away from the noise and the rich odors of human sweat, manure, and frying meat. She wanted to stand in front of the ocean and gaze into the waves, but she was on the wrong side of the island for that.

She stopped and leaned against a post, clutching her basket against her side. She checked on Pietr, tucked snugly in the basket. His little eyes were open, but he wasn't fussing at all. His small chest rose with each ragged breath.

A man walked by, grinning at her. She didn't return the look. With a quick motion, she wiped the sweat off her face, and made herself move forward, despite the weakness in her legs. She had never been this weak and tired before. She wondered if it would ease.

Inside, Dreamland rose around her, almost shutting out the sky. Wide buildings dominated streets decorated with incandescent lights. Elephants walked past her, their gray flesh stinking of rotting meat. Around a corner, people gathered before a fence, watching native African tribes playing in the dirt. Rose stopped for a moment, but a young boy, naked except for a cloth around his waist, stared at her with such despair that she walked away, feeling guilty somehow for the boy, in a wide-open cage far away from his home, living his life in full view of mean and curious spectators.

Other huts and makeshift villages stood off on side roads, people gathered around them. Rose avoided them. Here the air smelled of smoke, and she heard the clang of fire bells. Down a nearby street, a building burned as part of the entertainment.

She had gone to hell, just as her father said she would. Hell and beyond. But it didn't matter. For her father knew nothing of where she was. He was working his little farm in the Midwest, a thousand miles away, raising the other, better children. She was here, with Cousin Louisa, until the disgrace passed.

Disgrace. Pietr was not a disgrace. He was little and innocent, and he was dying.

Delighted screams rose off to her left, but she ignored them. Instead she walked through the narrow streets until she saw the sign she had been looking for.

It stood atop a Swiss-style building that looked as if it could have come from the Midwest instead of New York. People poured in and out, talking animatedly. Rose stopped, her heart pounding in her chest. The midwife had said to come here. But it seemed so silly, with people on display, fake fires, and all the screaming. Down the street, devils perched on top of buildings, calling out to passersby. This did not look like a safe place, a place that could help her or Pietr.

But she had come this far, and she had to get the baby out of the heat. She walked up the two wooden steps and let herself in the front door.

The air was dry here, cooler, smelling faintly of milk and something else, something metallic. People stood in small groups around metal boxes that leaned against the wall. Rose joined a group, looked through the glass, and saw a baby, tiny as her Pietr, lying in a bundle of blankets, a thermometer hanging above his head, and another, official-looking gauge beside him. A woman was speaking to the crowd, talking about families of incubator children, children raised in their own private castles, like royalty.

The basket was heavy. Pietr's eyes were open, watching her. She smiled at him, and then put her fingers against the glass case. Children she couldn't touch. On display, like that little boy in the African exhibit.

"I'm afraid, miss, we don't want you touching the glass." Rose turned, and found herself looking down at a woman wearing a nurse's costume with a starched white collar.

"I didn't come to see the babies," Rose said. "I came to talk to somebody—" Her legs wobbled beneath her, and she had to grab the woman for support. The woman took Pietr from Rose, then put her arm around Rose's back, and led her into a side office.

"You all right, child?" the woman asked. She set the basket on the table, touching Pietr lightly, moving the blanket from his chest.

Rose wiped her face again. It felt wonderful to be off her feet. "Do you have water?"

The woman nodded and disappeared through a door. She came back with a full glass, and watched as Rose drank it.

"How long ago?" the woman asked.

Rose looked up, saw the understanding and a bit of pity. "Yesterday."

"You shouldn't be walking, child, on your own. Isn't there someone you could have sent?"

Rose thought of her Cousin Louisa, with her thick German accent and wide bosom, negotiating the sins of Dreamland.

The nurse shook her head. "I suppose if there were, you wouldn't be here. I'll get the doctor."

Rose closed her eyes for a minute and felt the dizziness ease. The nightmare wasn't over yet. It began two days ago, more than a month early—"God's punishment for your sin, young lady," Cousin Louisa said—pains shooting through her bloated body, and a baby pushing to emerge. Cousin Louisa had gotten the midwife, and together they nursed the child from Rose, a little boy, Pietr, born too small and too frail to survive.

Except, the midwife said, a man in Coney Island could help her. The hospitals won't work with him, but he has helped hundreds of babies. Hundreds.

The baby, Cousin Louisa intoned, would die for its mother's sins.

All night she had sat awake, watching her baby struggle for each breath. It wasn't right that he would die because she and Gustaf had explored each other in her father's apple orchard. Pietr didn't ask to come to her. And her father wanted her to leave the child with Cousin Louisa. Louisa, who thought Pietr should die.

"Miss?"

Rose opened her eyes. A man stood in front of her. He was as tall as she was, with white hair and wide sad eyes. He went over to Pietr and held out a finger. Pietr watched, but didn't move.

"How early was he?"

"A month," Rose said. "The midwife said you could help."

The man took Pietr from his basket, and held him against his chest. "Maggie!" he called. The nurse came back in. "This baby needs attention."

The nurse took Pietr. Rose rose, but the man put his hand on her arm.

"He needs to be changed, and to have something to drink." The man's voice was kind. "We won't do anything that you don't want us to."

Rose sat back down.

"I'm Martin," the man said. "I'm a doctor. I developed the incubators."

"Rose."

"Do you know why the midwife sent you to us?"

"She said babies that young don't survive outside of the womb." Rose blushed at the words. "She said you could help."

"I put babies in incubators like the ones you saw out there. They stay warm and protected. They get fed, and they're safe from the dust and the dirt of the world, just as they would be if they remained inside their mother." He leaned forward. "How old are you, child?"

"Sixteen," Rose whispered.

"And you're not from New York, are you?"

She shook her head. "I can't pay you. My father—"

"I know, child," Martin said. "That's why we're here. The fees we get from the people viewing the babies help mothers like you."

The nurse brought Pietr back in and handed him to Rose. She wrapped her arms around him, felt his warm, fragile little body. His eyes remained closed.

"I have to leave in two days," she said. "My Cousin Louisa is supposed to raise him. But she says he's supposed to die because I sinned, and I can't leave him with her. I can't. But she'll take him back, if she knows where he is."

Martin glanced at the nurse. She shook her head slightly. "We can't keep the babies," he said. "Pietr's your responsibility."

"I was thinking," Rose said, arms tightening around Pietr, "with all the people coming through, that you might see someone who wants a baby, someone who can't have one and will give him a good home. I can't, and Louisa can't, and otherwise he's going to die—"

"Your cousin doesn't know where you are?" Martin asked.

Rose shook her head. "And I have my train ticket in my pocket. She bought it for me yesterday to get rid of me, so she could take care of Pietr."

Martin touched Pietr's head, and Pietr turned, just a little. "Stay here tonight," he said. "Decide in the morning." Then he took his nurse's arm and they left the room.

As the door closed, Rose heard the nurse's voice raise. "Martin, we can't broker babies."

"And we can't let them die—"

The the door latched, and the voices faded, leaving Rose alone with her firstborn son.

• • •

In 1958, Rose and Henrich fly to New York City. They have never been on an airplane before, have never left the Midwest before. They cling to each other as the plane bumps through the air, and they let out a sigh of relief as it returns to the ground. Their son got them reservations in New York City, and they take a cab to their hotel. In the morning, they will take a train upstate to visit their son, his wife, and their three children.

But that afternoon, Rose insists that they go to Coney Island. Henrich doesn't understand, but he doesn't resist.

Coney Island is not the land of her dreams. The amusement parks are gone, except for Steeplechase, looking old and beaten by the sea. Laughter echoes, but not the gay laughter of her imaginings, a dark, almost sinister laughter she sometimes hears in her sleep.

Henrich wants to go on the rides, but first Rose walks to the ocean. She stands at the edge of the water, feeling it lap against her corrective shoes. She is sixty-seven years old, and hasn't danced since her only daughter's wedding. Sometimes, late at night, she sits alone and listens to the phonograph of "Dreamland," letting the images swirl in her brain.

She half expects to see him, walking tall among the waves—for he would be tall. Gustaf was tall, she was tall. He wouldn't be handsome, not in a young sense, but he still would have beauty, to her. He is fifty-one years old, and probably not called Pietr. The postcards from Martin never said.

She can still remember the first: *He is fine—one of our successes!—and will move in next week with a young lawyer and his wife from Manhattan. He is a beautiful child.* She burned it, like the others, until they stopped, just after her daughter's birth, in 1926. She knew they would stop, because the newspaper carried Martin's obituary. She recognized him from his likeness, and his pioneering work at Dreamland.

And when her daughter's youngest spent his first week of life in a hospital incubator, she thought about her trek to Dreamland, and how Martin had finally achieved his dream.

"Rose?"

She turns, wanting to see Pietr, but instead seeing Henrich. He has grown stout over the years, his hairline receding and his nose expanding to fill his face. He was never beautiful, like Gustaf, but he was kind. He never said anything after their wedding night, although he had given her a measuring look. And two years later, when Cousin Louisa had told him the truth, calling Rose a sinner and a fallen woman, Henrich had thrown Louisa out of the house for failing to respect his wife. Then he had come up to Rose, shown her how much he loved her, and gave her their own son.

Their own son. Whom she loves with an abandon she has never felt for Henrich. Perhaps she loves the boy enough for two sons. She picks up a handful of sand and lets it run through her fingers, cooling, gentle.

Coney Island is not what it was, and neither is she. But in her mind she can still see Dreamland. She can still hold tiny Pietr, and she can still dance.

She reaches out a hand to Henrich, and as he pulls her forward, she laughs. He stops and looks at her with amazement—when was the last time she laughed with such joy?—and then he pulls her in his arms and laughs with her.

Their feet aren't moving, but Rose and Henrich are waltzing. And the towers of Dreamland rise ghostlike behind them, across the shimmering sands.

# Somewhere in Dreamland Tonight...
## Madeleine E. Robins

THE DRESS, WHEN SHE FINDS IT, IS PINK. It smells richly of lavender, slightly of camphor, an uneasy mixture in the stifling heat of the attic. Ruth sits back on her heels and holds the thing out before her wonderingly. From the style, it would be from before she was married, when she was still living with Aunt Min; the summer she was wild, going out to Coney on the weekends with that girl from her office. She imagines herself in the dress, poised before a mirror.

A door slams downstairs. Peg, on her way out to God knows where. On the surface of the cloth Ruth sees the argument an hour before, her daughter standing in the attic doorway shouting that she is old enough to run her own life. "I bring home my pay, don't I? I'm entitled to a little fun. You just don't know the way things *are*." Sees herself, all the love and worry she feels turning to hard little words in her mouth when she tries to caution her only child, her baby. The headache that began an hour ago dances hotly behind Ruth's eyes. Her eyes and throat itch.

Ruth shakes the dress out brusquely. Why did I keep it, she wonders. There is yellowed lace at the collar; on one side there is a small brown stain, almost invisible. When she looks at the dress Ruth feels a frisson of fear and something she almost doesn't recognize: a sudden unnerving sexual pang. That was the summer that ... she begins, then cannot finish the thought. Memories of that summer are immediate, but something eludes her. Did something happen? She tries hard, going beyond the heat and dust in the attic, beyond the pain that makes her vision jump with each pulse; Ruth knows the dress means something, but cannot recall what.

The summer when she was wild, she calls it in her memory. *But what we thought was wicked then.... I always went home with—what was her name? Leda McHale—back to Leda's to sleep on the trundle in Leda's own bedroom, as chaste as a nun.* I should go downstairs now, she thinks. But downstairs will be empty of Peg, gone off to a football party at the college. Downstairs will be full of Peg's discarded stockings and teddies, the purple cloche hanging off the newel post the scent of Peg's too strong, too suggestive perfume. Peg doesn't understand. She's too young—what's eighteen years? *She* doesn't know how men can be. Ruth knows.

• • •

The dress, when she found it, was pink. It hung in the window of Hooley's Dry Goods and Ladies' Furnishings and cost Ruth almost a week's wage from her job as a type-writer. The bodice draped to a short waist, the sleeves teardrop-shaped with lace at the wrists; the collar was ivory lace and rose high, high on the throat, to just under her chin. In it Ruth, with her soft, rounded chin and strawberry blonde hair, looked like an illustration from the *Home Journal*. The mirror and the salesgirl both told her so. She bought it knowing that Aunt Min would purse her lips at the price.

On Saturday, early, she donned the dress, pinned her hair up under a small, flirtatious straw hat, and told Aunt Min she was going on a picnic with a friend from the 17th Street Methodist Church choir. Then Ruth was gone, gone to meet her best friend Leda, Leda's brother Jonah, and Jonah's fiancée Pearline, to catch the train to Coney.

Going to Coney. It was forbidden fruit; Aunt Min read the *Police Gazette* with as much fervor as her Bible, and knew chapter and verse about the vice and depravity practiced at Coney: men and women clinging to each other on the great wheel, five-cent beers, freak shows. If Min had known where Ruth really intended to spend the day she would have locked her in her room and read temperance lectures to her through the keyhole.

The train ride felt endless. In the heat Ruth's hair began to come down in rosy wisps, sticking to her cheeks and neck. She dabbed ineffectively at the beads of perspiration on upper lip and brow with a handkerchief, stealing a glance at the other women in the car. All of them were flushed and moist, languorous in the heat. Leda and Pearline giggled and poked at each other and at Ruth; Jonah slept through their mirth with his boater drawn down over his eyes, the tips of his waxed mustache gleaming in the sunlight.

When they got off the train it was all spread before them: Steeplechase and Dreamland, Luna Park, the grand old resort hotels down the coast, the Boardwalk. Revitalized by the freshening breeze from the water, Leda and Ruth immediately wanted to run ahead. But Pearline wanted a lemonade, and to sit in the shade with Jonah. So Ruth and Leda sipped lemonade and tried not to listen while Jonah and Pearline whispered to each other on their side of the table. Ruth was astonished at their shamelessness, but no one else seemed to notice or care. Leda caught a man staring at her, and when she frowned he tipped his hat and smiled, and Leda started to giggle. At last, with lemonade still sticky on their lips, they left the stand for the parks.

For hours they rode the rides, squealing at every bump and whirl and breathtaking turn. Pearline nestled against Jonah, shrieking until he tightened the arm that circled her waist; Leda and Ruth clung to each other in delicious terror. Under the grinning supervision of Tilyou's great clown they gorged themselves on up and down and sideways motion. Then they went down Surf Avenue to Luna Park to watch the Great Naval Spectacular, arguing which park was the best. Leda and Jonah liked Steeplechase; Pearline preferred Luna's uplifting spectacles. Then, at dusk, they came to Dreamland, and Ruth knew which park was her favorite.

• • •

The clock downstairs strikes five o'clock. Ruth starts, looks up, remembers that Peg is gone and that Peg's father won't be home from the lodge until late. She has the house to herself tonight, big and empty.

They have done well, they own the house outright, even have a broker and stocks; Peg went to a good school for young ladies across town, and Ruth has a girl in three times a week to help with the house and do the heavy cleaning. It is more than she ever dreamed of, growing up in Brooklyn. The house is big, the girl won't come again until Monday, Peg has gone out against Ruth's wishes, travelling with that fast crowd, college boys. Why can't Peg understand? What is it that drives her out to parties, sends her home after midnight with gin breath unsuccessfully disguised with peppermints? But even as Ruth thinks "I never…" the dress in her hands belies the thought. She can remember the thrill of sneaking out, doing the forbidden, going to the forbidden place. More: when she looks at the collar she remembers the way it circled her throat so that her chin nestled in a ruffle of lace. Remembers tilting her head until it was cupped by the lace as if it were a firm, cool hand. Remembers the hand tracing a path from her ear down along her throat, slowly and caressingly. Abruptly she looks away.

· · ·

The dress, when she found it, was pink, jumbled in the corner with half a dozen other garments, its soft fabric creased and dotted with greasy spots, a clump of dust clinging to the fold of the bodice. On the high lace collar, so tiny one could miss it, a stain in the shape of a perfect droplet, rusty red. Ruth shook her head, trying to remember what it meant. It was hot in her room, stifling, and the sunlight brought on a headache as she looked at the dress. Something.... Aunt Min bustled in to borrow a pair of gloves for church and saw Ruth's headache written clearly across her face. Then it was a matter of cool compresses, Aunt Min's assurances that the Almighty would excuse her missing Sunday services this once. Min herself drew the shades and dabbed at Ruth's temples with lavender water until Ruth wanted to scream. Finally she went off to church, the feather in her hat standing righteously erect.

The dress still hung over the back of her wicker armchair. As she stared at it a whisper threaded Ruth's memory: *rose pink lady*. Who called her that? With each glance at the dress the sense that she should remember was fainter, less imperative. At last she got up and hung the dress in her clothes press and lay down to wait out the headache.

When she awoke it was dusk, and the week stretched before her like a quiet road at twilight.

· · ·

The world went away when you entered Dreamland and there was nothing but light and music and people everywhere. They went first to the Venetian Canals, where Pearline and Jonah rode the gondola, heads close together with the boatman's uninterested chaperonage. Then Leda wanted to see the midgets; Pearline wanted to see Creation. Ruth didn't care: everything was fine with her in Dreamland.

As they walked along they were hailed by the barker from the Congress of Living Wonders. Jonah shook his head and pulled Pearline after him. Leda followed. Behind them, Ruth looked over at the platform for a moment. She was about to turn away when she saw a man looking at her. She blinked and he tipped his hat and smiled. He must mean some other girl, she thought. But she hung back, delighted and appalled to realize that he *was* looking at her. Of all the women in the crowd he chose her to smile on. In the swirl and eddy of the crowd Ruth stood rock still, looking at him.

He stood a few feet behind the barker, near the curtain at the back of the platform. He didn't seem to have a part in the show; he was simply observing. Ruth was so rapt, so fascinated by the dark sparkle of the man and the flush of excitement that made her blush, that she didn't see Leda and Jonah and Pearline continuing on to the Creation pavilion, pushing through the crowd as oblivious to her loss as she was to their absence.

He was dark and polished, like an onyx pebble. His pearl grey suit was fresh despite the heat, his tie and collar crisp at his throat. His eyes were dark as onyx and his smile had a cool, white light all its own. From the platform the barker spoke insinuatingly, drawing the crowd in to see the Bearded Lady, the Man with Two Mouths. As she pushed forward with them, searching for a coin in her pocketbook, a hand at her elbow stopped her. He was there beside her, the onyx dark man, saying "Keep your money, darling. It will be my pleasure."

Blushing, Ruth let him guide her into the show. Light from the incandescents flooded the area unevenly, leaving dark pockets between the exhibits; they gave a low sizzling noise which blended into the calls and sighs and shrieks of the crowd and the performers. They paced leisurely from one platform to the next as the barker's feverish baritone extolled the strangeness of this one, the awfulness of that. Ruth listened with half an ear, distracted by the presence of the onyx man at her side. His light touch on her elbow that kept her constantly aware of him, his heat and scent and male presence.

They strolled past the freaks and wonders and Ruth accepted each of them without question because they were dressed in his glamor. He murmured softly into her ear until she giggled nervously at his comments about the fat lady's beard and the sword-swallower's wrinkled tights. His breath was hot in her ear, moving the strands of her red hair against her cheek. When they came to the show's end and the barker exhorted the audience to Come Again, Come Again, Ladeees and Gentle-men, the stranger leaned close. "Rose-pink lady," he murmured. "Will you take a walk with me?"

Then they parted from the audience and left the hall by a doorway in the rear, their passage noted by the barker with a knowing glance. Her onyx-dark man led her through an alley and out into the main street, and they sauntered like any other summer beaux in the crowded lamplight. A sudden turn just past the Hellgate, down an alley, and then he brought

Ruth through a door and into a dusty vaulted room. It was dim after the glare of the street; Ruth blinked owlishly. She could make out wooden struts and draped canvas. There was a strong smell of paint and varnish and moldy sawdust. Ruth turned toward the man only to find him there beside her, very close. He traced the bow of her upper lip with one long finger, a gesture which shocked Ruth and moved her in a way she could not understand. When she closed her eyes she could feel his breath on her ear again. Inside her something like Aunt Min's voice scolded, told her to run quick.

"Rose-pink lady," he murmured again.

Ruth didn't move, except to tilt her face up to his.

• • •

Leda was waiting for her at the Beacon Tower.

"Where've you been?" she fluttered. "Jo and Pearlie are looking for you everywhere, we thought you were lost. Ruthie, you all right?"

Ruth smiled and nodded and said she'd just lost them in the crowd. "Did you see the midgets?" she asked.

Leda shook her head. They had been searching for Ruth. Jonah was fit to be tied.

"We'll have to come out again," Ruth said softly. "There is so much to see yet."

Then Jonah and Pearline found them. Ruth endured their scolding all the way to the train station, and until they boarded the car back to Flatbush Avenue. She slept on the trip back, stumbled into Aunt Min's flat, got herself to bed somehow. Already she was thinking of next Saturday.

• • •

The next time it was all familiar: the parks, the paths that connected from one to the other. The excitement that traced pathways along the nerves when you first stood there at dusk surrounded by the lights and the smells and the sounds and the tastes and the people. When they reached Dreamland Jonah took Pearline and Leda off to the Midget City and they agreed to meet at the tower at nine. Ruth had told them she was meeting a friend from her church choir. Jonah may have believed her; Pearline and Leda winked broadly and took him away before he could ask too many questions. Helping Ruth each girl borrowed a little of her adventure, thrilled to their own illicit part in her drama.

From the gates of the park it took Ruth only a few minutes to find the Congress of Wonders. By the curtains at the back of the platform she saw him, dark and polished. His smile gleamed in the dusk, and Ruth's pulse began a slow, dramatic hammering. He knew she had come to find him, she knew he knew. Everything would move forward now from that knowledge.

He took her elbow and guided her forward, smiling solicitously.

"I don't know your name," she heard herself say. His eyes were very dark.

"Adam," he said quietly.

This time he did not take her to the backstage of Hellgate. Instead they walked a thread through canvas tunnels, alleys, under the boardwalk and out onto the beach. The ocean , overshadowed by the parks, glistened in the moonlight. He held Ruth's fingers in his own cool, dry hand. After a while they took their shoes and socks off and walked with the sand between their toes. They talked, then were silent.

When she met the others at the Beacon Tower later she walked slowly, as if her blood had taken on the rhythm of the sea. On the long train ride back to Flatbush Avenue Ruth's hand floated at her chin and caressed the lace collar of her dress.

That night she slept at Leda's. Her dreams were full of darkness and rhythm, the touch of his hand, of his lips.

. . .

What is it about the college, about those boys that Peg finds so attractive? Ruth frowns in the dimness of the attic. *I should turn the electric on*, she thinks, but doesn't get up to flip the light switch. Those boys, most of them cheap, stupid. They have raccoon coats and cheap Ford autos and Peg thinks they're exciting. She'll waste herself on one of those boys, break her heart. None of them will stay with her, marry her, take care of her. She doesn't understand what I want to spare her.

Under her hands, which clench and twist, the fabric of the dress tears slightly, releasing more lavender scent on the air. *The summer I went to Coney*, she thinks. *Over and over, every Saturday all summer long, with Aunt Min wondering and worrying and never saying a thing, just looking down her nose on Sunday mornings when I came home from Leda's.* She stares at the dress in her hands and slowly smooths the creases away.

• • •

During the week Ruth was quiet and thoughtful. She did her work quietly, didn't spend much time talking to the other girls in the office. She browsed the shops looking at dresses, but she had a superstitious feeling about wearing any other dress than the pink one out to Coney. She went to choir rehearsal on Tuesday nights, and helped with Aunt Min's Friday socials. pouring out weak tea for hours without protest. She carried her secret like an amulet against boredom and frustration; it took so little to recall the feelings of Coney, the looseness and languor, the hot urgent pressing of his lips against her throat. On Saturday mornings she woke up, really awake, and dressed in the pink dress again, and went to meet Leda and the others for the ride out to Coney.

After a few weeks, Leda suggested they go somewhere else on Saturday. To the country for a picnic, to the city for a show. Ruth smiled and said perhaps, but each Saturday they went to Coney. Pearline saw her fill and more of the miracle babies and Jonah watched the end of Pompeii until he was sick of it, but as long as they could sit in a gondola or on a wooden horse, pressed together, they were willing to go out to Coney again. Leda looked out for young men looking at her, but none did, no matter how she giggled and flirted her eyebrows. As the summer went on Leda giggled less. Ruth didn't share her adventure with Leda, forgot to ask if Leda had any beaux or flirtations. Leda, who had always been the forward, kittenish one, began to look confused and hurt. Ruth did not notice.

August turned chilly for a few days; Aunt Min took her mantle from the back of the closet to wear for church, and Ruth took to carrying a shawl with her. On a Wednesday at the office, Leda told Ruth that she and Jonah had a christening to go to that weekend. "We'll have to go to Coney next week," she said, not bothering to hide her satisfaction.

Ruth panicked.

She went through the day thinking *how can I go out there?* For a moment she thought, *maybe Pearlie will go with me.* But Pearline would probably go to the christening. Even if she didn't Pearline would never allow herself to be abandoned at Dreamland while Ruth went off on her own. As she transcribed pages of manuscript on the typewriter her mind was at Coney with him. How could she get out to Coney? She even thought *perhaps Aunt Min?* No, not until Hell froze over, maybe not even then. The more she thought, the more it seemed that she would really die if she couldn't get out to Dreamland on Saturday. Her thought was rattled by the pounding of the typewriter under her fingers. After a while even Saturday seemed too far off. What would he think when she didn't come? Would he forgive her? Would he smile on someone else? Ruth imagined his beautiful smile for someone else. She had to tell him she wasn't coming, that it wasn't her fault or her idea. All afternoon the feeling grew strong, so that fear fed more fear, and she couldn't stand it that she wouldn't see him *tonight*, tell him everything, how Leda and Jonah and Pearline and Aunt Min were trying to keep them apart.

At six o'clock when she left the office with the other girls, Ruth turned left instead of right. Leda, waiting for her a few steps away, called after her.

"Ruthie, whererya going?"

Without turning Ruth called back, "You know where I'm going."

• • •

*What happened that summer?*

The thought catches Ruth by surprise. What is happening to Peg right now, that's more important than what happened twenty years ago on a beach miles away. The answers seem intertwined to her, they stand on each other's shoulders, if she can answer the one she'll know the other. *Why did I keep this dress?* The answer comes: *to remind me.*

*Of what?*

• • •

The train wasn't full, but there were still people, even families going out. Ruth felt they were looking at her, all alone with no friend, no chaperone. She pulled her shawl tighter around her and clutched her pocketbook in her lap. What would she say to him? At the sight of him she knew her doubts would melt away. Everything would be all right when she saw him. She twirled a strand of hair around her finger and stared out the window toward the nearing glow of Coney's lights.

When she got off the train it was all familiar but different. Fewer people, fewer families. More young men lounging on the benches, eyeing her, calling out Hello, Sweetheart and Looking For Me, Girlie? Even inside the gates of Dreamland everything felt subtly wrong , the music too sharp, the lights too bright, the laughter too coarse and familiar. For the first time Dreamland was not an enchanted village but a playground, loud and vulgar. She thought, it's not a dream, it's a nightmare.

He wasn't at the Congress of Wonders. The barker saw her, all right: tipped his bowler and smirked, and then pursed his lips in a soundless whistle as if he knew something she didn't. She began to push her way through the crowd into the freak show; the barker didn't try to stop her, no one demanded money. She just pushed in and pushed through, ignoring the freaks, looking for a dark head, a white smile. When she came out the exit she pushed on to Hellgate. All the places he had taken her, the backstage areas, the cul-de-sacs between rides and exhibitions, even the shadowy path under the Boardwalk were hard to find, although she had thought she knew them.

When she reached the beach at last she was exhausted and bedraggled. The hem of her brown twill skirt was soggy and stained, and her white shirtwaist was creased and dirty. She held her hat in one hand; it had come off when she climbed under the stanchions of the Boardwalk. *Where are you*, she prayed. *Please find me, please.*

In the moonlight the ocean looked like a flat, tranquil mirror. A hundred feet away she saw him, grey and silver in the moonlight, his back to her, looking out at the ocean. Ruth gasped in relief and began to cross the sand. He turned at the sound and she saw: there was a girl in his arms, pale and fair, her face turned up to his. What was worse, Adam's face when he saw Ruth was perfectly blank, as if he didn't know her at all. No fear, no explanation, no surprise. He was as smooth and implacable as an onyx pebble.

Ruth turned and ran.

They found her at the Beacon Tower, waiting for them. When Jonah put his coat around her shoulders and Leda took her hand to lead her out of Dreamland, Ruth smiled and cried, as if she was too grateful to them ever to stop smiling, and too miserable ever to stop crying. She cried like a child, and felt like a child, pathetic, small and weary. When they got her on the train she slept all the way back, waking fitfully to clutch at Leda and weep again.

They brought Ruth home that night over her protests. Aunt Min's icy disapproval vanished when she saw her niece's grey, miserable face. Leda and Min put her to bed with a hot water bottle and a cool compress, and Ruth fell back into her restless sleep. Her dreams were full of darkness and rhythm, of pulses and heartbeat, the touch of Adam's white hands on her, the weight of his body leaning in to her; she dreamt of his breath cool in her ear, loosing a hot churning excitement in her belly and between her legs. His lips, tracing a path from her ear to her throat. His teeth, nipping gently, then piercing. Their cries, together, as he took from her and she gave, yielding everything up to him. His teeth at her throat, piercing neatly, releasing a flood of liquid heat through her arteries. It was everything she had heard of love: he told her it would only hurt once and then only pleasure, only joy.

The same joy she had seen him giving another girl in the shadows cast by the lights of Dreamland, the blood a black smear across his lips.

She woke early the next morning. The sunlight was white on the counterpane, unavoidable. Carefully folded on the chair by her wardrobe was the pink dress. For a moment on waking, Ruth remembered it all, everything. Then, as if it were blood seeping from an unseen wound, the memory began to leech out of her. Finally her recollection of Coney, of the whole summer, was as white and stainless as a bone.

When fall came Aunt Min packed the summer clothes away with lavender. In the spring, sorting through them, Ruth saw the pink dress, shook her head, put it back in the trunk. Not a style that wore well. That winter, in December of '09, she met Peg's father. Dreamland burned down in '11 and all that was left were the Coney Island waltzes she danced to at her wedding: "I'll see you somewhere in Dreamland, somewhere in Dreamland, tonight..." Ruth became a wife, then a mother. The Great War came and went. She had a home, a family, a good life. The past shimmered in her mind as elusively as the lights of Coney Island, lost in the sunlit now.

· · ·

A crash from downstairs. Startled from her reverie, alarmed by the series of thuds and crashes that are Peg making her way up the stairs, crying out wordlessly for her mother's attention, Ruth hurriedly bundles the dress up and shoves it back in the chest. She blinks in the light of the upstairs hall and closes the attic door behind her.

"Peggy?" She calls down urgently. A slurring voice answers, tells her to go away. Ruth follows the voice to the bathroom, where Peg is angrily scrubbing at her collar.

"Don't start with me, Ma." Peg refuses to meet her eye, stares resolutely at the mirror as she pokes angrily at a red stain on her collar.

Ruth stands for a moment, transfixed, the bottom dropping out of the world, everything, everything coming back to her in a flooding rush of memory. "What happened, baby," she asks like a prayer. Trembling, she brushes Peg's hair back, away from her face and away from her throat; sees the white, unmarred flesh. The memory is replaced by a surge of relief so powerful she wants to cry. Ruth does not pursue the memory but gathers her daughter into her arms, rocking silently.

Peg resists briefly. "Don't start with me, Ma! You were right, all right? He got drunk, he started grabbing at me. I hate him, all right? Isn't that what you want me to say?"

"No, baby, no," she says. "Hush, hush, it's all right now." Every hard thing Peg says is forgiven; Ruth thinks, *You don't understand. You can't understand. You don't know how men can be.*

Ruth knows.

# Doctor Couney's Island

## Steven Popkes

IT WAS DAMNED COLD THAT MORNING. You never thought Coney Island would ever be that cold. All you ever thought about the Island were the lights, bright like Fourth of July sparklers, and the smell of crowds and spilled beer, hot dogs and sauerkraut. And it was funny, he mused for a long minute, lying on his side on the frozen sand. Funny, you never remembered the smell of the ocean but here it is, as sudden and surprising as flashpowder: salt and the ripe stink of dirty water. What was the ocean more than that? Merlin rolled himself up and leaned back against the clapboard wall of Dreamland— No it wasn't. Dreamland burned down years ago, burned down, oh the bright lights of that fire!, and was rebuilt by somebody new, died a financial death and was buried in the middle of Steeplechase. Where *was* he? He'd been nearly fifty when that happened. How old was he now?—and looked out over the water. His stomach hurt, a hard, unyielding knot. The flat land and calm sea looked as if they were drawn on paper. It was early morning just before the sun rose and the sun's breezes bit, as small and sharp as small dogs. Merlin huddled in his torn coat at their expectation.

• • •

(The beach on the Normandy coast was always cold. A hard wet sandy beach that matched him, hardness for hardness, when he stepped off the boat. A hardness in me at leaving. A hardness in me at being forced to leave. Arthur, I thought. You're on your own.) He shook his head. He was trying to remember something. The beach. He was somewhere on the beach—near Nathan's down from the boardwalk. They came here last night—who?

• • •

Jimmy the Pinhead was lying next to where Merlin had been sleeping. Merlin slapped him on the rump. "Wake up," he said. Then coughed up a fluid mess, spit it on the sand and eyed it curiously. He shivered as the sun flared over the sea. Baths, he thought. I remember the baths—was that ten? Twenty years ago? Before John McKane died.

Warm, they were. Hot. Steamy.

"Wake up, damn it." He kicked Jimmy viciously in the foot.

"Leave a sick man alone." Jimmy groaned and pushed him away.

"We stay here much longer and we won't be sick." Merlin leaned over him and shouted in his ear. "We'll be dead."

Jimmy put both hands over his ears and sat up. "You're a filthy old man."

"You're right about that."

"You hurt my foot."

"Stop whining or I'll break your head." Merlin shivered again. "We got to get somewhere warm."

"There any more liquor?"

Merlin stood and stretched, coughed again. "Yeah. French champagne. Come on."

He half led, half pushed Jimmy back up over the boardwalk and down the alley towards Asa's place. As the breeze rose Merlin felt even colder and there were moments of sharp panic when Merlin couldn't seem to remember how to breathe—leaning against the closed storefronts.

Jimmy waited for him, patient as a drafthorse. Finally, Merlin brought them into the warm crook created by the space between Asa Morse's flower shop and Bond's Nickel Beer.

"This is warm, Merle." said Jimmy, sniffing the air. "Smells nice, too."

Merlin didn't answer. He huddled with his back against the brick wall of the flower shop, feeling the warmth of the coal furnace seep slowly into him. It loosened some glutinous substances deep in his chest and he was wracked with deep, painful coughs. Blackness edged his vision and everything he saw had showers of colors. Merlin had a sudden image of himself turned inside out. Then, the coughing passed and he felt the cold mentholated air filling his lungs.

· · ·

(The air in Salem had been sweet, each breath like a labored symphony as I struggled to lift my chest one more time. Trapped with a mountain lying across me. I wanted to cry out I that was no witch. Cry out that I was, after all—just for a clean death. Either admission would destroy my children. Instead, I stayed silent, trying to breathe, wishing I could just die. I heard a voice ask me to confess—to what? Ravings? Had I breath and inclination I might have laughed. Had my body less strength I might have died right then. Neither happened. Only my breath, sucked against too much weight and leaving too quickly.)

What was it he was trying to remember?

. . .

Someone took his arm, placed it across his shoulder and hoisted him to his feet.

"Stupid," Asa Moore said as he helped Merlin into his shop. "You were always stupid. Now no better than when you were a kid."

The sunlight seemed brighter in the greenhouse in the back of Asa's shop, reflected from rows of lilies and camellias, budding now but not yet bloomed. And it was steamy warm as when John McKane had taken Merlin and other ballot box enforcers to the baths on the night of the Coolidge election as a reward for faithfulness.

. . .

(Steamy, as when I'd sat with the Emperor and we'd been talking what to do with the Senate. "They'd be useful as goats. Not otherwise." he'd said and I had agreed.)

. . .

Asa took Merlin's head in his head and brought his face close.

"It's me, George. Asa Moore."

"I know you. I was just thinking."

Asa let him go. "Good. You get crazier every year."

Merlin shook his head. "I'm not crazy."

"Of course not." Asa spun around and grabbed Jimmy by the neck. "Damn you, don't touch the flowers."

Jimmy snatched his hands back and held them under his arms. "I'm sorry. I was just trying to smell them."

"Go sit over there, next to the furnace."

Jimmy sat on the bench in the corner and in a few moments was asleep.

Asa snorted. "At least, he's easy."

Merlin nodded, sleepy himself. The smell of the budding camellias had a hypnotic effect on him. "Best pinhead act on the island."

Asa smiled sourly. Such a great achievement." He rubbed his chest. It's too much work carrying you in here. My heart isn't what it used to be. I have to work too hard as it is—two thousand carnations. Three hundred lilies. A hundred camellias. Them, I have to take care of. Otherwise, I don't make it through the year. You, I leave to freeze next time."

"Guinevere loved camellias. I did, too, for that matter."

"Shut up with that crap. You can stay here and keep warm but I don't have to listen to that King Arthur crap."

"He's Merlin," said Jimmy, suddenly awake. "He told me."

"Crap." Asa stood up, short and furious. "His name is George Thomas and he grew up in Gravesend the same as I did, before it had hotels or amusement parks. We fought over the same girl. We worked for McKane together, keeping his tax collectors and prostitutes in line. George's been drinking himself dead since before you were born. I've seen it for forty years right into the middle of this Goddamned depression. You think I don't know who he is *now*?"

Chastened, Jimmy huddled back down on the bench. "And you." Asa said, turning to Merlin. "Don't tell me flowers. You know how I know you're crazy? 'Cause there were no camellias in King Arthur's time—not there. Camellias aren't native to England. A goddamned florist knows these things. They were brought to Europe. Long, long after your great king."

• • •

(Short, like Keaton is short, standing on the field when the house fell down, so convinced of his own skills, of his planning, that when he stood there, serene as a saint, I had to look away. I've seen the last of him, I thought. He's dead, sure. And we all turned away—even his wife, a slight and pretty thing—and heard the crash and turned back and he was standing, looking at us. And in that moment, we could all read his mind as sure as if he'd shouted at us: "Did you get it? Was the camera rolling?" And all we could think was, "How did you *do* that?")

That's not it. It was something else.

"Some other flower, then. Something like camellias. Asa, you don't understand." Merlin rubbed his face with his hands, suddenly aware of the smell of his clothes, the ancient sea smell of his skin. How much could Asa know? Merlin remembered listening to pronouncements and whimperings across the night wind when he was a child. Listening, rapt, to everyone still living, to those that had died. Was there any wonder he was confused? "It's like?" he groped for words, feeling the leftover remains of alcohol like wool in his thoughts. "It's like we can all remember each other. Like remembering dreams."

"Crap!" shouted Asa beating the air with his hands. "You started this crap when McKane went to jail and we had to hide out in Jersey. It was crap then and crap now."

"He's all the time, fulla' crap." came a thin voice behind Asa.

Asa turned around and let his arms fall, rubbed his chest with one hand and nodded. "Yeah. Hi, Joe."

Joe Littlefinger stepped down into the greenhouse, smoking a cigar as thick as his wrist. Joe's wrist, like the rest of him, was diminutive. He was slightly over three feet tall, but every inch of him was dressed impeccably: vest, jacket and pants, gold watch chain and derby. He knocked ash off the end of his cigar into one of the lily pots.

Asa reached down and gently plucked the cigar from his hands. "Later, when you go outside. I have enough problems without you killing my flowers." He reached through the door and placed the cigar outside.

Joe nodded, imperturbable. "Sure, Asa. I'm going up to Doctor Couney's place to look at the kids. Any of you guys want to go along?"

Merlin looked at him. "They're closed up. No tours until spring."

Joe shrugged. "I'm feeling generous today. One of the nurses will let us look at them for a half a buck each."

"I don't even have that."

"I'll spring for everybody." Joe waved his hand at them.

Asa had flowers to take care of and Jimmy had fallen asleep again. As Merlin followed Joe out the door, Asa grabbed his arm.

"Don't make me bring you in again, George." he said. "You come on in and sleep next to the furnace. You'll die if you stay out there."

"Thanks, Asa."

Asa looked deep into his face, grimaced. "You won't do it. I'll find you huddled next to the wall outside, dead, one day."

Outside, the cold had sharpened but with the sun stronger now, it didn't feel quite so close. Joe retrieved his cigar carefully from the stoop and lit it, puffed it in glorious satisfaction.

"Life's worth living if y'got a good cigar, eh?" Joe tried to blow a smoke ring. The light breeze defeated him and he shrugged.

Doctor Martin Couney's Premature Baby Incubators had once been a featured attraction of Dreamland. But Dreamland was gone and the babies remained, now down the Bowery from Asa's shop. Joe and Merlin walked quickly to get out of the cold.

"Say, Merle," said Joe matter-of-factly as they walked. "Jimmy tells me there's something to this magic stuff of yours."

"There is no such thing as magic." said Merlin shortly. A sudden breeze down the street made him shiver. "I know."

"Not the way he tells it."

"Jimmy's a pinhead."

Joe nodded. "What's the truth, then?"

Merlin shrugged. "I don't know."

"Come on. Don't clam up on me."

"I don't know what it is. We remember each other. That's all. That's all I've ever said. Asa thinks I'm crazy." Merlin stopped in the middle of the road and stared down at Joe. "Do you think I'm crazy?"

Joe inspected the end of his cigar. "I think you were smart when you were with McKane and then you started drinking too much and talking too much. Now you're a bum."

Merlin laughed. "That's honest." He stood up straight and looked around him. The sky was a light turquoise and there were gulls flying overhead on sun-gilded wings. He held his arms wide. "I remember Arthur as a child—when the Romans left England, running off when the King fell. People dying—a thousand men in an hour. Can you imagine that? I ran. I remember the Romans, marching up big, wide roads—better roads than we got here, f'Christ's sake—into France. But we didn't call it France then. I don't remember what we called it. But I remember watching them. I remember marching with them. I remember marching with the Redcoats through Concord—I remember a lot of marching. I think I remember the Pharoahs—but it gets hazy that far back. Like remembering when you were three. I remember—"

"Right, Merle. Come on." Joe took the edge of his coat and started to pull him down the street. "Let's get out of the damned cold."

"I remember it all."

"Yeah?" Joe spit on the ground. "Right. I should have known. Asa said you grew up together as kids. He says he should have known it then:

you're crazy as they come." He strode ahead quickly, his feet striking the ground like small hammers.

"I said I remember it."

"Just like I remember being that son-of-a-bitch Charlie Stratton, too." said Joe viciously. "And his bitch Lavinia. I'm thirty-eight inches. Four too many inches and fifty years too damned late. I could have made meat out of him. He was *so* genteel. I can sing. I can dance. I can play the fucking piano. You know hard that is with these fingers?" He held up his stubby hand.

Merlin stared at him, bewildered. "What are you talking about?"

"I'm talking about show business, knucklehead." Joe slapped his arm. "'Tom Thumb is my *stage name*,' he said. Like there was something else. I had my name changed. I don't give a cobbler's piss I was born John Quincy Armont. Joseph Littlefinger *now*."

"What?"

Joe stopped in front of him and in a sudden unexpected display of strength grabbed his jacket and pulled Merlin to his knees. "I'm talking movies! Jimmy said one of these ghosts of yours makes fucking movies! In California."

"Christ," moaned Merlin, and started laughing. He fell backwards into the street, sat down heavily. "You want an introduction?"

"Yes, goddamn it. Stop laughing."

But Merlin was coughing and spitting and laughing on the ground.

"Stop laughing." Joe said again, took a long pull on his cigar and breathed out a great cloud of smoke. "It's a stupid idea."

Merlin gasped for breath and sat up. "Not really. It just doesn't work that way. I don't know any of these people. I just remember them—as if things happened to me. I don't even know their names."

"Right. You're a bum and a drunk and an ancient magician." Joe chuckled wryly. "But even a blind pig in shit will find an acorn sometime. And like the hedgehog said to the hairbrush, you can try anything once. Get up. Let's go see the babies."

Merlin felt obscurely stung to be so blithely cast aside. "Maybe I can figure out who he is. He works with Buster Keaton."

"Never mind."

"We're all related somehow—maybe we had the same ancestor somewhere."

"Adam No-navel, no doubt."

"Look, I didn't ask to have this happen to me." Merlin shouted at him. "Did I? I *liked* John McKane. I was happy working for him. This stuff eats away at you. It's not my fault."

Joe gently took his arms. "'Suffer the fools', they say. Come on, Merle. John McKane's been dead for thirty years. Coney's answer to Boss Tweed died before I was born. And Midget City was never what it was cracked up to be. It's been a whole new world for forty years."

"You think I'm crazy."

"Who isn't? I come up to your waist. Makes me a little crazy, too."

Merlin still felt sore. "Then, how come you're always inviting me along?"

Joe grinned at him. "How tall am I?"

"How the hell should I know?"

"Exactly." said Joe. "Come on. Let's go see the babies."

· · ·

(A baby is always small. The hand cradles the child's head easily. Perhaps God shaped men's hands for this purpose and this purpose alone, I thought, holding my son in my arms. All other possible uses for them are but happy accidents. Lie still, little one, I croon. Lie still and sleep. Perhaps some day you will be great carpenter.)

What was it he was trying to remember?

· · ·

There were six incubators in the room, large white enamel and glass cabinets, each with its impossibly small infant contents. Here was a little girl, her hands the size of thumbnails. Next to her was a bluish boy, his chest no bigger around than a cup, struggling for breath. The breath goes in, the breath goes out.

The nurse smiled at Joe and looked dubiously at Merlin, but let them both in when Joe gave her an additional quarter. They walked past the different children until Joe stopped before one small, swollen-eyed child.

"You have to meet Billy." he whispered. "Billy Watterson, meet Merlin the Magician. Merle, meet Billy."

"Hello, Billy," whispered Merlin. Billy was no more than skin covering cords and veins. He was smaller than the others, no bigger than a Nathan's frank. Merlin pressed his face against the glass so he could hear the boy's tiny breath. Straining, he heard the faintest rustle of leaves, the mere ghost of breathing.

"I like the tyke." said Joe softly. "He's less than two pounds—but Couney says you can't tell what he really weighed when he was born. They lose weight so fast, he said."

"Mister Billy Watterson, welcome to Coney Island."

They stood together in silence for a long time.

"You know," Joe said slowly. "This is his island."

"Billy?"

"No. This is Doctor Couney's island." Joe put his hand on the glass and leaned forward to see if the baby would respond. The baby seemed too intent on breathing to pay attention. "You and I are just so much air. McKane died. Tweed died. Dreamland died. Luna Park's dying. Steeplechase will die someday. And no one will remember them or us. But they'll remember Martin Couney and these little incubators. And the babies that live here and grow up, strong and tall. People will remember them and forget us."

Merlin shook his head. "No. It won't be like that. They'll remember the lights and the rides and the spectacles and the fat ladies and the strong men and the beaches and the crowds and Nathan's hot dogs and the freak shows. But Couney and his babies they'll forget."

"You're a drunken bum," Joe snarled at him softly. "What the hell do you know?"

Merlin grinned and tapped his skull. "Crazy, too. Merlin has second sight, doesn't he."

The nurse came in suddenly. She pointed at Merlin. "You have to leave. Doctor Couney knows Joe, but he doesn't know you. He doesn't like to have his nursery cluttered with smelly, drunken bums. Now get out of here."

"Who's smelly?" chuckled Merlin.

"Go on." Joe pushed him. "I'll catch up to you later."

Outside, the air had warmed and it was almost noon. He wandered over behind Nathan's to rummage in the backalley cans for lunch. He was lucky. There was a half pound of moldy cheese and some buns only partly soggy. Sometimes he wondered if the cooks at Nathan's were leaving food out on purpose. He walked back up Twelfth street and back under the boardwalk to eat. Merlin scraped the cheese against the corner of a brick piling and tossed the wet portion of the bread out to the gulls. In a small protected area, the sun shone on him and reflected from the walls and he was almost cozily warm. He savored the cheese and the bread and the resulting full stomach, and drowsily asked the air for a bottle of wine. The air was unmoved and he fell asleep.

Some long time later, he felt a rough hand shaking him rudely awake. Merlin sat up, blinked several times and rubbed the gum from his eyes. It was Joe, sitting on the sand. Wordlessly, Joe handed a bottle of cheap brandy over to him.

"What's the occasion?" asked Merlin. "Not that there needs to be one."

"We are drinking," said Joe ponderously, "to the late William Watterson."

It was a moment before Merlin knew who Joe was talking about. "Oh, no," he said when he understood.

Joe nodded. His clothes were dirty from walking under the boardwalk and there were deep gouges in the leather of his shoes. Joe did not seem to notice. "Mister Watterson, after a valiant effort at the very basics of living, quit this mortal coil about an hour ago. Doctor Couney tried to persuade the young man to stay but to no avail. Mister Watterson was adamant. This was no world for him."

All Merlin could think of was the tiny sound of the baby's breathing, imagining the faint, almost imperceptible cough, the deepening strain and then a deep sigh and silence. He rubbed his face with his hand, then tipped the bottle up and drank.

"To young Billy."

"To young Billy. We hardly knew you." echoed Joe as he took back the bottle. "Christ, Merle. He was so little and he tried so *hard*. I never knew anything so small could work so hard just at breathing." Joe looked as if he was going to weep, as if, for a moment, he was a child himself. "The kid deserved a rattle, or a ball—or at least a tit, like a normal kid. Not a glass box and a little coffin. The best we can give him is a good drunk."

· · ·

(As I lay on the bed, each breath was life bubbling to me through the fluid in my lungs. I was drowning—hadn't I heard once that drowning was an easy way to die? The man who wrote that was lost in an opium dream. "Gladly live, gladly die…" Did I write that? I never dreamed the last moments would be so hard. The body doesn't die easily. It dies hard—it fights for every breath, every heartbeat. Until, like coal burning, the ashes overwhelm it.)

That was almost it.

· · ·

Merlin found tears on his own cheeks and wiped them away. He sniffed and that brought on another coughing attack, each building from within to an explosive climax, like nitroglycerin in his lungs, priming the next until there was no breath at all, just a one long ragged wheeze.

Joe held him as he fought for breath. "Don't die on me now, Merle," Joe moaned. "I just couldn't take it. I swear, I just couldn't take it."

The cold air finally filled his lungs and he breathed carefully, as a thirsty man is careful with water. When he could, Merlin sat up and drank some of the brandy, feeling the warmth in his throat soothe his lungs, put a fire in his belly and a rubbery strength in his arms and legs.

"I left Jimmy over at Asa's shop. I got to go over and check on him. Asa's always scared he'll break something." Merlin stood up and dizzily leaned against the piling.

"Yeah." Joe drained the bottle and threw it viciously against the piling. The glass exploded and Joe stared at the wet spot. "Poor little son-of-a-bitch. I'm going to go home and get so drunk I can't sit in a chair." He looked up to Merlin. "You come on by if you don't want to sleep under the boardwalk. You always were good drinking company. Good company all around."

Merlin looked down at the sudden compliment. "Yeah. We'll see. I don't know where I'll end up."

"You think about it. It gets damned cold out here." Joe straightened his suit, pulled out a cigar out of his pocket and lit it. The fetid smell almost made Merlin throw up.

Joe tipped his hat to Merlin and started walking down the beach towards Steeplechase. Merlin watched him for a moment, then ducked back under the boardwalk back to Twelfth Street towards Asa's shop.

· · ·

(It was a measure of my stature as a physician that I would be called to treat someone such as Harry Houdini. The escape artist had proven difficult to treat not because of the injury—which was, in fact, terminal—but because of Houdini's personality which I found abrasive and made worse by his great pain. Still, it was hard not to feel pity as the man was pulled inexorably towards death. Houdini's pact with his wife, to come back after death, struck me as pitiful.

"There is no magic." Houdini whispered when we were alone. He looked about the room as if his wife would hear him.

"I know." I said, remembering everyone who remembered me. "More than you do." )

I know I'm looking for something. I know that. Desperately, completely. I want to know what it is.

• • •

He met Jimmy on the Bowery next to where the corner of Dreamland used to be.

"Hi, Merle." Jimmy said affably. He jerked his head towards Asa's flower shop. "He didn't look to good, so I thought I'd go home."

Merlin stared for a moment towards the shop, then searched Jimmy's slack face. "How'd he look."

"Real tired, Merle." Jimmy shrugged. "I thought Gunther'd give me some wine if I came back on my own. He was real pissed the last time he found me under the boardwalk with you."

"Okay. You go on." He pushed Jimmy up the street. "I was just coming to get you."

"You have any wine?" asked Jimmy wistfully.

"Not a drop. But Joe does."

Jimmy nodded. "I'll go see him."

With that, he turned and walked steadily up the street, placing his feet with careful exactness. Merlin, watching him, was reminded of the time he and Jimmy had gotten drunk and the pinhead had fallen and broken his knee. Jimmy must have decided to be more careful from that, or had it pointed out to him. It wasn't clear Jimmy was smart enough to figure it out for himself.

Asa had fallen asleep in his chair in the shop. His broad face lay on his chest like a deflated child's ball and snored faintly through his nose. His face was gray and chalky and he looked shrunken in his sleep, as if pulling away from a deep and abiding pain. Asa's heart had been troubling him for over ten years and Merlin knelt next to him and peered closely, trying to see if Asa's heart had begun to fail at last.

(Arthur had already heard the songs being sung about him as he lay on the bed. The King looked bad. His face was white and the continual, constant pain had given his voice a whimpering quaver that I hated. He hated it more than I, especially the craven sound that lurked in it when he asked for drugs.

"I never wanted to die." he said through clenched teeth. "Always, I feared it."

"No man is different." I said and leaned close to him, cradled his head against my breast. Once he had taken pleasure in that touch but now it was mere consolation.

"You cannot cure me, eh? Not even of the pain." He tried to chuckle but it sounded bitter. "You are not much of a witch."

"No, my love." I said looking down into his eyes. "I never was."

"Give me another damned potion then."

I held his head as he sipped it. "It is spring." he said after a moment, as if that were some great surprise. "Can you smell the camellias?"

He did not speak again and soon after we laid him amidst the flowers he loved.)

•   •   •

"Maybe they weren't camellias." Merlin muttered under his breath. "Just because I remember them there doesn't mean they weren't there, does it?" Or did it? He remembered the smell strongly, as strongly as he could smell it here, now, in the greenhouse. A mistake in memory, maybe? Did that turn the whole tapestry of mind into rotting cloth?

The flower smell in the greenhouse was overpowering. Asa did not rouse as Merlin watched him. For the space of a hundred breaths, Merlin remembered his own life, not the others. Remembered he and Asa growing up in Gravesend, growing corn and squash, watching as the first hotels were built down on the beach, watching Norton build his bar and gambling den and begin the building of Coney Island. He remembered the whores on Sheepshead Bay and the night John Y. McKane tried to keep his empire against the entire state of New York by protecting the ballot boxes with a mob of Irish thugs. Merlin had been there, had wielded a club against the state-appointed voting supervisors. So had Asa. And hiding up in Harlem for two months waiting to get caught as McKane's trial dragged on and on. Impatient, running from New York into New Jersey, waiting again, following the trial, following the hearsay up and down the coast, trying to find out if it was safe to go home. He remembered working with Asa bucking hay on a horse farm, telling him one day in a moment of weakness about the voices and flinching away at the confusion in Asa's voice. Then, later, when they were both drunk, trying to explain. He'd been trying ever since.

His memories since McKane were faded like old cotton, the past bright as flowers. Even so, Asa was always there. Asa and his carnations, caught up in the idea down in Jersey and coming home to make it happen. Marrying, birthing, dying, all those things mixed together in Asa's life and Merlin watched it from under the boardwalk, like some ancient bridge-confined troll, watching people glitter through the planks, the light of the world reduced to slits Asa slept. His breathing was labored. Stealthily, Merlin unbuttoned Asa's shirt and rested his hand on the bare skin. A warm smell compounded of earth and sweat escaped from the cloth.

Now, he prayed. If there is no magic, there can be no harm done in this. But if there is—and my life says there might be—heal this heart. Take my own heart for his. I never thought there was a God as the priests told me. Prove me wrong this once.

Out beyond him, residing in the ether like small eddies in a great river, he felt them there, dead and living.

He listened to them for a sign, a hint of what to do. All he heard was the sound of the sea. It was as if he were standing in the water with high tide rushing past him, eyes closed, hands in the ocean, overwhelmed, and when the tide had turned, he looked down in his hands to see what had left him.

• • •

(At last, I felt something give inside of me. The breath went out, the last of the good Salem air, and did not come back. And for a long, suspended moment, as I waited for it to return, knowing it would not, I realized that which had given way was life, and with the life the pain. There was no pain in dying. There was only the pain of holding onto life. I must remember this, I thought in sudden fever. I must remember.)

I remembered now.

• • •

Merlin pulled his hand away from Asa's chest and carefully and gently replaced the cloth. He sat back and watched him for a long time.

Asa roused and blearily looked around the room. His gaze fell on Merlin. "Hey there." He straightened up. "I wasn't feeling too good so I sat down. I didn't mean to take a nap. What time is it?"

Merlin shrugged. "I don't know. It's late. It'll be dark soon. How do you feel now?"

Asa stretched experimentally. "Better, I think. I don't feel any pain, anyway. For me that's good news. But then, it comes and goes. You don't look so good."

Merlin shrugged again. "There's nothing new in that." He stood up and swayed a moment, felt his heart stab with a sudden pain.

"Are you okay?" Asa stood up and steadied him.

Merlin nodded. Smiled. "Yeah. I'm fine. I think I'll go down to the beach. I like the water."

Asa scowled. "You'll end up getting drunk down there and freezing to death. If it doesn't happen tonight, it'll happen later. Come on back here. Where it's warm."

Merlin shook his head.

"Christ! All those famous people you say you remember. Isn't there one ordinary person that has some sense?"

He chuckled, suddenly weary. "I'm a bum at Coney Island, Asa. What do you want me to do? What the hell else have I got?"

Asa softened. "Come on back. It's cold out there."

He looked at Asa, watched the small face as wrinkled as an old apple. "Maybe you're right, Asa."

Asa took him by the arms. "You aren't a young man, George. Come back here and stay warm."

George. He tasted the word. It had been a long time since he had thought of himself with that name. "Maybe I will. But I still want to go down to the beach for a while."

"You wouldn't disappoint an old man, would you?"

"Not if I can help it."

The wind died as the sun faded behind Steeplechase. The longest shadow was that of the parachute drop, two hundred feet tall, a long, skeletal umbrella. Dark now against the light. Lit again, Merlin knew, in only a few months.

He stood in the middle of the beach and watched the boardwalk turn charcoal black until there were only the silhouettes of things: the roller coaster, the shuttered freak shows, the Ferris Wheel. Behind them, he could see at that moment, the lost towers, minarets and battlements of Luna Park and Dreamland, and behind them, again, the lost palaces and castles of Africa and Araby. Behind them, at last, he could see the memories of his own life, all of them, and adding to them now his own.

Pain shot through him, lancing his life like a scalpel across a boil. He coughed so long an hard that there was thunder in his ears and he forgot how to breathe.

There is no pain in dying, he remembered, proud that this salient fact had stayed with him. And he held this thought as the dark came towards him.

That night, across the cold ether of the world, there were the faint and intermittent sounds of mourning and remembered death. And, if one were quick, the smell of camellias.

# One Million Light Bulbs

*Lawrence Watt-Evans*

JOHN CHESTER GLATFELTER stared at the newspaper in astonishment. "Is this right?" he demanded. "It's not a typesetting error?"

Charlie Beckett, Glatfelter's personal secretary, glanced over Glatfelter's shoulder to see where his employer was pointing.

"One million electric lights," he read aloud, "Illuminate the splendors of Dreamland."

"One *million*? They can't really mean that."

"I think they do, sir," Beckett murmured. "I've heard the figure before."

"Twenty years ago there weren't a million light bulbs in the entire city of New York! Now they've got that many in this one silly playland?"

"So it seems, Mr. Glatfelter."

"How can they afford it?"

Beckett shrugged—not obviously, more to himself than to his employer. "I understand that Mr. Reynolds raised a considerable sum of money for the construction of Dreamland," he said. "I believe it was more than three millions of dollars."

"Reynolds?" Glatfelter turned to glare at his secretary. "*Bill* Reynolds? Is that scoundrel behind this?"

Beckett pointed to the fine print at the bottom of the newspaper advertisement. "Mr. William H. Reynolds," he said.

"If that don't beat all," Glatfelter said, squinting at the tiny type. "What's Bill Reynolds doing, messing around with playgrounds out the hind end of Brooklyn?"

"Well, sir," Beckett explained, "Mr. Tilyou's Steeplechase Park has been such a success that it's inspired others. Last year it was those two showmen, Thompson and Dundy, with their so-called Luna Park—they spent a million dollars and used two hundred and fifty thousand electric lights. So this year Mr. Reynolds has gone them one better, and opened Dreamland, for more than *three* million dollars, and with a hundred thousand lights on the central tower alone, a million in all." He hesitated, then added, "It's quite a spectacle, sir."

Glatfelter turned again. "You've been there?"

Beckett cleared his throat. "Yes, sir. I've taken my girl Polly out there three or four times now."

"I'll be damned," Glatfelter muttered. "A sensible fellow like you, wasting your nickels on Coney Island?"

"Yes, sir. It's really quite enjoyable."

"Amazing." He stared at the newspaper for a long moment, then announced, "Beckett, if they're even getting people like *you* out there, then there's money to be made—and I'll be damned if I'm going to let that fool Reynolds make it all, while I'm left out!"

· · ·

"Noisy," Glatfelter said. He looked around critically. "Is this the best place you could find?"

"Yes, sir," Beckett said, nodding, and trying not to stare at the stranger Glatfelter had brought along. "You'll understand, most of the owners on Coney Island aren't interested in selling; they find it quite profitable. This is the only location where I could put together a decent parcel of land."

"Well, it'll have to do, then. Not the best spot, but when we're done it'll look like a glimpse of heaven." He frowned. "We can dig a channel to the sea there," he said, pointing, "And put our lagoon just there, with the tower behind it."

"Ah... you're planning a lagoon and tower, sir?"

Glatfelter turned and glared at him.

"Beckett," he said, "Does Luna Park have a lagoon?"

"Yes, sir."

"Does it have a tower?"

"Yes, sir."

"Does it make pots of money?"

"Yes, sir."

"And does Dreamland have a tower?"

"Yes, sir."

"And does Dreamland make pots of money?"

Beckett hesitated, and Glatfelter continued without waiting for an answer. "Of *course* we'll have a lagoon, and a tower, and everything the other parks have, and we'll make it all bigger and better! That scalawag

Reynolds probably thought he'd topped Luna Park so completely he'd put it right out of business, with his million light bulbs, but he ain't seen nothing yet, my boy! Dr. Petworthy and I will show *him* a thing or two!"

"Dr. Petworthy?"

Glatfelter gestured at his silent companion, a cadaverous man wearing a worn black frock coat and a flamboyant black mustache. "*This*," Glatfelter explained, "Is Dr. Emil Petworthy, the world's foremost expert in the physiology of fun!"

Beckett blinked.

"Good heavens, boy, you didn't think I'd come out here blind, did you?" Glatfelter shouted. "I'm planning to invest ten millions of dollars in Miracle Park—I'm not going to just throw that away!"

"Well, no..."

"So I went to the University—to Columbia—and I asked 'em who was the top man in the science of enjoyment, whatever the hell they called it, and they talked for a while, and then they sent me to Dr. Petworthy, here, the world's top authority on phallicology..."

"Felixology," Petworthy corrected, in a nasal squeak.

"Whatever."

"I see," Beckett said. He stared in dismay at the self-proclaimed felixologist, with the horrible suspicion that the faculty at Columbia had played a cruel joke on his employer firmly embedded in his mind.

"Dr. Petworthy," Glatfelter explained, "Has determined that it's the electrical machinery that makes these parks so much fun for the lower classes."

"What?" Beckett's stare shifted briefly to his employer, then back to Petworthy.

"Yes," Petworthy explained, "It's the electrical fields. They affect the brain, you see. All those electric lights create what I call a euphorogenic field—they create a feeling of lightness, a pleasurable sensation. Naturally, the more refined and trained senses of the educated classes are less susceptible, but the working classes obviously enjoy it very much indeed."

"Right," Glatfelter said. "It makes 'em happy. So we'll put our tower right *there*, with a million light bulbs on it, and Dr. Petworthy will wire it up to make the biggest, strongest you-forget-it field in history..."

"Euphorogenic."

"Whatever. Those others, Tilyou and Thompson and Reynolds, they did it by accident, whatever they may think; they still don't know that these electrical fields are the *real* reason their customers are so happy. *We* will do it on purpose, we'll give the customers a taste of paradise, and as for those others, we'll run 'em all into bankruptcy court!" Glatfelter chuckled.

Petworthy grinned, a hideous, skeletal grin.

Beckett licked his lips nervously and didn't say a word.

• • •

"You don't need all that stuff," the electrician said, pointing at the tangle of brown-cloth-wrapped wire, the chunky solenoids, the oddly wound coils.

"I know," Beckett said, "But follow the plans."

"It's a waste," the electrician insisted. "That dope Petworthy, he don't know anything about wiring. Thinks he's Dr. Tesla or somebody."

"I know," Beckett repeated, "But Mr. Glatfelter wants it done just the way Dr. Petworthy says."

"It's gonna pull current like nobody's business," the electrician warned.

Beckett rubbed his head, which was starting to ache. "Just do it, will you?"

"Putting a million lights on this tower —you know, the way it is now, when the micks come to America and sail into the harbor, first thing they see is the light from Coney Island. Mr. Beckett, I swear, when you get this thing working they'll be able to see it without leaving Ireland. Mr. Edison's gonna be rolling in dough. You'll need a half-dozen men working full-time just to replace the ones that burn out."

"Just do it and shut up," Beckett said.

The electrician shrugged. "You're the boss," he said, turning away.

• • •

"But Mr. Glatfelter," Beckett said, "You *can't* open with the place like this!" He waved one arm in a sweeping gesture that took in the half-finished cyclorama of "Moses in Sinai," the "Palaces of Babylon" scenic railway that had yet to make a run without a car jumping the track, the workmen repainting the façade on the House Of A Thousand Delights for the fifth time.

"Sure we can," Glatfelter said. "The season's starting, we don't want to miss Memorial Day."

"But Miracle Park is *not finished!*" Beckett insisted. "The customers will be disappointed."

"No, they won't," Glatfelter gloated. "Dr. Petworthy says the tower's all ready to go."

"But the *rides* aren't, the *exhibits*—you've had everyone working on that tower and the lagoon, and…"

"That tower's all we need to make Miracle Park the biggest money-maker in America!"

"Mr. Glatfelter, nobody's going to pay money just to see a million light bulbs!"

"They'll pay their dimes to feel good, boy, for something that'll take them away from their worries for a little while, and that's what Petworthy's machine will do for them!"

"Have you *tested* it? What if Dr. Petworthy's theories don't work?"

"Of course they work!"

"Have you *tested* it?"

Glatfelter glared angrily at his subordinate. "No, we haven't tested it," he said, "Because how *can* we test it, without a crowd of customers?"

"You could see how it looks," Beckett suggested desperately. "The sun's setting, you could see how it looks. You could see how it affects the workmen."

Glatfelter rubbed his chin, considering that. He threw a glance sideways at the tower—a replica of the Leaning Tower of Pisa, built somewhat larger than the original, painted every color of the rainbow, and with a steeper slant that Petworthy claimed would enhance the effects of the euphorogenic field. Every visible surface was covered with light bulbs, and Beckett knew that the interior was jammed full of wiring and machinery, most of which, the electricians all agreed, would do nothing except draw current and maybe overheat. In fact, three electricians had walked off the job, claiming the thing wasn't safe, and the fire marshal had needed a bribe almost three times the going rate.

"Sure," Glatfelter said. "Turn it on and let's see how it looks." He grinned. "It'll look like a little bit of heaven, Beckett—all that light, those colors—you'll see."

Beckett smiled with relief. He was sure that Miracle Park could work, could make money—but as a legitimate amusement park, not because of Petworthy's crackpot theories or crazy machinery. Probably the best thing that could happen would be if the tower burned itself down right now.

"Joe," he called, "Turn on the tower lights, would you?"

The foreman, who had been lounging a few paces behind the big shots, looked up. He turned and looked at the tower, leaning out over the lagoon, bristling with clear glass spheres and brightly painted arches.

"Not my job, Mr. Beckett," he said nervously.

Beckett's smile vanished. "Do it anyway. Or you won't have *any* job."

Joe sighed, and headed for the switch-house by the main gate.

A moment later, he called back, "Here she goes!"

A low whine sounded, and with a sudden blaze of incandescent brilliance, one million light bulbs flared into life; light and color exploded across the lagoon and courtyard of the unfinished Miracle Park.

Everyone blinked, closing their eyes against the sudden glare. Hands flew up to shield eyes, and the men squinted.

"Bright," Beckett said. It seemed, in fact, much brighter than even a million light bulbs ought to be.

"We just weren't expecting it," Glatfelter said, but for the first time in the four years since he had met Mr. Glatfelter, Charlie Beckett heard a tinge of doubt in the millionaire's voice.

Something popped, and hot glass sprinkled on the flagstones as a light bulb exploded. The whine rose slightly in pitch. Cautiously, Beckett turned to look at the tower through the slit between his fingers.

Bands of color seemed to be moving up and down the diagonal cylinder, and the overall glow was pulsing rhythmically.

"Mr. Glatfelter..." Beckett began.

The whine suddenly soared madly upward in both pitch and volume, becoming an ear-splitting scream; instinctively, Beckett closed his eyes and turned away.

The sound went up into the ultrasonic, where it could not be heard, only felt as a painful pressure in the ear; more light bulbs burst, and a fine spray of glass particles spewed out across the lagoon. The tower shimmered.

And no one saw what happened next; everyone there, from J.C. Glatfelter down to the merest workman in Miracle Park, had turned away from that unbearable brilliance. All they saw, through closed eyelids and shielding hands, was a sudden dimming.

And the pressure in their ears was gone; the sound had stopped.

Slowly, cautiously, Charlie Beckett uncovered his eyes and turned to look.

The tower was gone, and in its place...

He didn't really have words for it. It was like a bubble, or maybe a hole. It wasn't really there at all, in a way, and what he saw was not what had replaced the tower, but what he could see of what lay beyond it.

And what lay beyond it was a street—not one of the rowdy, cluttered streets of Coney Island, or any of the crowded streets of 1905 New York, but a gleaming black band between towering buildings that shone pink in the light of the setting sun. Women in strange tight clothing walked on one side of the street, and a glittering red machine drifted down the center. Flying things that were not birds sparkled far overhead.

And then it vanished, with a pop like another light bulb exploding, and the lagoon and courtyard were back, dim and pale in the gathering gloom of early evening.

"How'd it look?" Joe called from the door of the switch-house. "I know you didn't say, but the switch was getting hot and sparking, so I figured I'd better turn it off... Hey!"

Glatfelter stared at the empty foundation beside the lagoon where a moment before his tower had stood, and then slowly turned to face Joe.

"Where'd the tower go?" Joe asked.

Glatfelter glowered for a moment; then he turned to Dr. Petworthy.

"All right, Petworthy," he said, "Where *did* my tower go?"

Petworthy just shook his head and continued staring.

Beckett cleared his throat.

"Mr. Glatfelter," he asked, "Did you see it, before Joe turned it off?"

"I saw it," Glatfelter admitted. "I don't know what the heck it was, but yes, I saw it."

Beckett's mouth twisted wryly.

"Well, Mr. Glatfelter," he said, "You *said* that tower would show folks a glimpse of heaven..."

Glatfelter threw Beckett a startled glance. "*That?*" he said. "Ha! A glimpse of heaven? Some damn fool electrical mirage, like those nickelodeon shows." His eyes narrowed. "But you just might have something, at that. Petworthy, if Joe hadn't shut the electricity off, would we still be able to see whatever it was?"

"I don't know," Petworthy said, staring at the empty foundation.

"Well, why not?" Glatfelter demanded. "Wasn't that your you-forget-it field at work?"

No one bothered correcting Glatfelter's mispronunciation this time. Petworthy slowly shook his head. "No, sir," he said, "I don't know *what* that was."

"Well, whatever it was, I want you to build me another one, and this time we won't let it disappear on us!"

"Sir..." Petworthy struggled to get the words out. "Mr. Glatfelter... I can't."

"Why not?"

"Mr. Glatfelter—I made it up as I went along, to impress you. I thought the million electric lights would create the euphorogenic field all by themselves; the rest was just for show, so it wouldn't look too easy."

For a moment Glatfelter was utterly speechless, rising up on his toes and dropping back, rising up and dropping, blowing air out through his mustache. Beckett fought down laughter.

"Well, then," Glatfelter said at last, "You can make it up as you go along *again*, damn it, and you can do it until you get it right. And when you've got it right, we'll open Miracle Park." He rose up on his toes again, and a smile began to spread beneath his whiskers. "And we'll have an attraction like nothing else," he said. "We'll show them all how it's done, we will—we'll make George Tilyou look like an amateur, Thompson and Dundy like dabblers, Reynolds and his flunky Gumpertz like fools. A glimpse of heaven!" He grinned. "One million light bulbs, illuminating a glimpse of heaven!"

• • •

Throughout the 1906 summer season Miracle Park stood closed and dark while workmen rebuilt the tower, and only incidentally continued work on the other rides and exhibits. Steeplechase Park and Luna Park and Dreamland took in millions of dollars, while Miracle Park earned not a single cent on Glatfelter's seven million dollar investment.

In 1907 Elmer Dundy died, and his long-time partner, Frederic Thompson, began to lose interest in Luna Park. Thompson's drinking problem worsened, but Luna continued to earn money.

That same year, Steeplechase Park burned to the ground; George C. Tilyou, undaunted, charged a dime admission to the smoldering ruins and immediately began rebuilding. The new Steeplechase was bigger and better, but still, in its way, just as tacky—and more profitable than ever.

Miracle Park did not open; Dr. Petworthy spent the entire year experimenting with the wiring in the tower, but all that happened was that the light bulbs blazed brightly while the coils and solenoids soaked up incredible quantities of electricity without doing anything. The rest of the park was complete, but J.C. Glatfelter wanted his tower and its vision of Heaven, or the future, or Mars, or whatever it was.

"Miracle Park could make money without it," Beckett pointed out one afternoon, as Glatfelter glared up at the brightly painted tower. "Steeplechase never had any towers."

"The hell with the money," Glatfelter replied. "I want it to work!"

. . .

By 1908 attendance had dropped off at Dreamland, the spectacular wonderland with its million light bulbs. In fact, Glatfelter's investigators reported that it was losing money steadily.

"How do you explain that?" Glatfelter demanded, shaking the report under Petworthy's nose. "Your euphemisms aren't working!"

Petworthy frowned, then glanced up at the tower; a tangle of bare wire was woven through the upper tiers now. "It's not the lights that do it, after all," he said. "My earlier theory wasn't complete. It's something about the metal. It's that steel racetrack around Steeplechase that keeps it popular."

Glatfelter stared for a moment; Petworthy wandered off, back toward his tower, looking rather dazed.

Glatfelter let him go, then turned to Beckett. "You," he said, "I want you to go to Steeplechase, and Luna, and I want you to find out what makes them so much fun."

"Dr. Petworthy says it's the metal," Beckett pointed out mildly.

"Dr. Petworthy is a complete loon," Glatfelter snapped. "What does he know about fun? But he knows electricity, and he made that tower thing work once, so maybe he can do it again. And meanwhile, I want YOU to learn about fun."

"Well, I don't know, it isn't part of my job and I don't see how I could do it alone..."

Glatfelter snorted. "I know what you're doing, boy. State your terms, then."

The haggling didn't last long. Glatfelter paid Charlie Beckett and his girl Polly five dollars a day to explore Steeplechase and Luna, trying to figure out what made them fun.

· · ·

Dr. Emil Petworthy disappeared mysteriously from his laboratory in 1909, and his whereabouts thereafter remain a mystery to this day. John C. Glatfelter, convinced that Dr. Petworthy had somehow once again opened an electrical gateway to another world, spent the rest of his life and his fortune hiring electrical experimenters in unsuccessful attempts to duplicate the feat.

Charlie and Polly Beckett tried for three years to convince Glatfelter to open Miracle Park, but eventually gave up. With the money they had saved and the knowledge of what makes people laugh that they had acquired at Coney, they moved to Los Angeles, where they made a fortune in the movies.

· · ·

In 1911 Dreamland burned to the ground, putting an end to Coney Island's spectacular era. No one ever seriously considered rebuilding; the manager, Samuel Gumpertz, instead opened a freak show on the site. Where Dreamland once stood is now the New York Aquarium.

Luna Park closed in 1946; Steeplechase went in 1964.

Miracle Park, John Chester Glatfelter's stupendous experiment in euphorogenics, never opened; the unfinished buildings eventually weathered away, and today an apartment complex stands on the site.

# Porthole Mirror

*Richard Coniglione*

SOMETIMES AT NIGHT, when it was very still, and the whirlpool flush from the toilet carried the condom away and dissolved into silence, I thought I could hear it. It was a small sound, similar to the gentle rush of a seashell cupped over your ear. That's what it sounded like, a tiny, far-away ocean. I told Donna about it and she laughed. "It's the real ocean," she said. "It echoes off the buildings and through the alleys."

Donna and I were practically engaged at the time. That's why I was living with her, even though I didn't much like the neighborhood. "It's funky," she said. "It's like the Village in the sixties. Now artists can't afford the Village. Only yuppie scum. Sort of like you." But her giggle was too innocent to be angry at.

We could move, I told her. We yuppie scum do okay. Which of course wasn't exactly true for me yet, but would be. And we could certainly afford a higher rent once I gave up my other apartment. "How about Bay Ridge?" I asked her. "It's near the water."

She shook her head. "It's all families. This is artists."

The only artists I'd seen were selling velvet paintings of Elvis or dogs, or Elvis and dogs, on Surf Avenue.

I listened, alone in the bathroom, as the tiny waves lapped back and forth, so quiet that no matter how carefully I turned toward the sound, the movement of my body drowned the noise and it was gone. It would not return no matter how long I continued to stand there, staring into myself.

The sound was coming from behind the mirror.

"Yeah, right," Donna said, smiling at me when I told her about it the next day. "Listen, we live two and half blocks from the Atlantic Ocean. It's just wind, pushing the sound out in front of it, up the blocks and down, and sometimes you hear it. Most of the times you don't, because there's too much other noise, but sometimes you do."

"No, it's coming from behind the mirror. I know what the ocean sounds like. I grew up on the island. The ocean doesn't sound like that."

Donna just nodded her head and went into the living room to paint. I stood in the bathroom awhile, listening to nothing. Then I shaved, using the porthole to see myself, dressed, and took the subway to work. It takes forty minutes to get from Coney Island to Wall Street in the morning. It seems like it should take longer.

Donna is from Canada. She is the first and only Canadian I've ever known. "Actually," she said, "we're a lot like Americans, only better. We don't think we run the world, we don't get pushy, and not only did we not kill all our Indians, we saved a lot of yours from you."

She looks like people from the Midwest, tall and pretty with high cheekbones and a slightly turned-up nose. She came to New York to study art at Pratt, which she said was a pretty good art school once, but she dropped out before she graduated.

"Artists don't graduate," she told me. "They learn what they can then move on. Right now I'm between teachers." But she told me that later, after I'd moved in.

When I met her, she was working the night shift at Nathan's, serving hotdogs and making change. I was reminiscing with some buddies over the fries. You can get Nathan's fries these days at franchises, but they never taste like they do at the original Nathan's. Some people say it's the salt air that changes the potatoes. I think it's the oil they use. They filled the vat in 1910 or something when they first opened and they haven't changed it since, only adding what boils away. They taste the same as they did when I was a kid. So once a summer at least we would go down and look at the rides and the lights and eat at Nathan's and get some cotton candy.

Except this time I saw Donna and it was late and cold and slow that night and she stood there with nothing to do so I offered to take her home, seeing as how the city just wasn't as safe as it used to be and figuring anyone who had to work nights with hot dogs and bums probably didn't have a car.

She laughed. "And how safe are you?"

"Depends. You want to see a driving record or a blood test?"

"Love in the nineties."

But she accepted the ride.

"Come back in a hour. My boss won't like it if you just hang out all night."

"I could just stand here eating hot dogs till you're done."

"Please. One or two of these I'll sell you. But if you want more you've got to go to another window. I don't want your death on my conscience."

The ride turned out to be a walk, because she lived in Coney Island, two blocks up from Surf Avenue in a run-down six-story walk-up. I sort of moved in three weeks later, leaving my furniture at my apartment in Brighton Beach, which was only a twenty minute walk. Maybe we would have moved into my apartment if I wasn't sharing it with Bob and things would have worked out differently, but I don't know. I took suits for work and jeans for weekends. Not much else of mine would fit in her closets. If this worked out I would talk her into moving to a bigger place in a better neighborhood.

Most of Donna's apartment was okay, walls painted white and everything normal, but the bathroom was a mess. It was the week before I moved in that it changed.

"Well, what do you think?" she said as she shoved me through the open door.

I was engulfed in a rush of blue and green, trying to force my eyes back into focus. I looked around the room slowly, hoping it would all make sense before Donna got impatient for a reply. Then everything fell together and I was standing on a small square island, surrounded by ocean and sky. It was like being on the inside of a magazine cartoon, with me the only castaway on a South Pacific atoll, accompanied only be a coconut tree.

The lower half of the room was still chipped grey tiles, but from chest height up the wall was covered by a three-dimensional wrap-around oil painting. The effect was somewhere between photography, painting, wallpaper, and laser hologram. The effect was also hideous.

"It's a seascape mural. I was up all night painting it. Do you like it?"

I nodded dumbly. The small room was enormous. The ceiling was filled with clouds and sky that moved down the walls to the horizon. It had no sun, only uniform brightness.

"You like it?" she said again.

"Yeah, sure, why not?"

"You're not just saying that are you?" Her hands were on her hips, slightly belligerent, and I knew I was going to have trouble convincing her. I also had the feeling that for the sake of this relationship I'd better convince her fast.

"Yeah. I like it. I mean why would I lie?"

She laughed. "Because it's horrible, that's why. And the reason you're lying about it is because you want to get me in bed and you're afraid if you hurt my feelings you won't."

"That's not true."

"Sure it is. But let's go. I want to see the movie and then probably we will come back here and screw all night, okay?"

Which is pretty much what we did.

"Why the ocean?" I asked her later.

"I need it. Canada's gorgeous, but it's all trees and farms. The ocean is power. That's why I came East."

"You could have gone to California."

She smiled. "Lucky for you I didn't. But someday I will, so be ready. Want to live in Santa Monica?"

"Sure."

Donna said the bathroom helped her paint. Whenever one of her funks threatened, she retreated to the bathroom for five or ten minutes and sort of meditated. I guess that's what it was. She was fine when she came out, smiling or whistling. My problems were shaving and getting out of the room. She had removed the medicine cabinet with its mirror and refused to put it back up. And the seams on the door were so unclear it was sometimes impossible to find the wall with the door, let alone the doorknob.

So the porthole made sense.

You see them all the time in stores, brass circles with a mirror where the glass should be. Nice decorations, if you like that kind of stuff, which I don't, but I figured that maybe she'd let me hang it because I was getting tired of having to feel around for nicks every day and then using the bedroom mirror to paste pieces of toilet paper over the cuts.

It was one of those hot summer days when I got off the train at Brighton Beach Avenue and walked the rest of the way, hoping the breeze off the ocean would be better than what was left of the subway's air conditioning. You come around from Brighton Beach right into Coney, passing the aquarium and watching the Wonder Wheel and rusting parachute jump growing to meet you, icons of a lost age. I stood for a while watching the merry-go-round spin, the only ride left on the north side of Surf, clunky music and two or three kids still grabbing for a ring that would win them a free ride. Donna said when she was little she would go the the county fair in Edmonton and take an outside horse, hanging off it like a nine-year-old Annie Oakley, grabbing the ring and riding round and round all day long. Riding in circles makes me sick, but it was okay to watch.

The rest of the block houses furniture stores and junk shops. They used to be arcade games, break the balloon, sharp-shooting, ball tosses. Now they were filled with tossed furniture. But hanging in one of them was a shiny porthole with a mirror in the center, perfect for shaving.

"How much?"

"Fifty bucks."

"That's crazy."

"Forty."

"I live around here."

"Okay, thirty. That's it."

I wasn't interested in thirty bucks, but I figured maybe if I gave him some time to think about it he'd come around. I headed to the back of the store and began poking around a dusty old bin of junk. In New York, this strategy works about half the time, the other half the guy figures out that you're still interested because you haven't left, so he sticks to his price. Economic chicken. It didn't work this time, so I bought the damn thing, had it wrapped, and put it in my briefcase.

It was just a lucky break that I was not carrying it when I walked in the door.

"Look," said Donna, dragging me back to the bathroom.

On the wall was a battered porthole mirror. It looked like an original porthole that someone had mounted a mirror in. And it opened, not like the new ones. It was a brass ring, surrounded by wood, and it was dusty and tarnished.

"I love it," Donna said, and I smiled at her. "It's real teak and it was only five bucks."

"It looks old," I said.

"Yeah. I found it on Surf Avenue. The bastard wanted twenty-five bucks for one of those new ones. I could have gotten him down to fifteen, I figured, but I hate them. They don't open and they're all brass and they don't need to be polished. You're supposed to polish brass."

Maybe I could get my money back. Probably I'd end up giving it to Bob for our old apartment.

She put it up in the bathroom and at least I could shave, though I couldn't see my whole face in it at one time. The porthole changed the bathroom from an island into a Flying Dutchman that would never see land.

It was a great going-away present, but not much of a welcome home.

Donna polished it to a brilliant shine until the wood smelled of lemon oil, happy, she said, to have to do it regularly. The only flaw, I thought, was the mirror, which was cheap. The backing had loosened over the years, I figured, and there was a lot of distortion. Not like a funhouse mirror, where the effect is comic. It was more like you see in a movie when they want you to think the character is crazy so they show you his face twisted just a little. I shuddered slightly and turned to Donna.

"Did you oil the hinge?" I said. The latch remained tarnished. I began fiddling with it, careful not to cut myself.

"Leave it alone," Donna said.

I turned. "What's wrong?"

"Nothing. I just don't want it opened."

"Why not?"

"I just don't, okay." She was silent for a time. "I'm afraid it's so old it'll break off."

I did not believe her, but she was set to argue. I shrugged. I think, for Donna, the noises behind the mirror had already started.

Donna was spending more and more time locked in the bathroom, especially at night. When she came out she was buoyant. Often she would come back to bed and ask for a hug.

The sounds that I heard continued for a few weeks, then abruptly ended, as if the water had retreated back to wherever it had come from. It was easy for me to forget the sounds. I told myself it had been the wind.

The only reminder was Donna. Her happiness wore thin as the sound faded away. Whenever she came out of the bathroom her mood was dark. She spent as little time there as possible, her oceanscape meaningless without the sound of her ocean. She talked a lot about swimming, obsessed with the sounds of surf, taking nighttime walks along the beach. I kept telling her it was too dangerous for her to be out alone.

"Come with me then," she said. "We can fuck under the boardwalk if you want." Something we were not doing in the apartment any more, I realized.

"I have to work tomorrow."

"Afraid you'll get mugged?"

"I have to work tomorrow, I said."

"Right."

Sometimes she was out until dawn. After first light I went to look for her and found her sitting in the sand, just staring out.

"I wonder if they're connected," she said.

"What are you talking about?" I did not sit down beside her. I was already in a suit and was holding my shoes and socks so they would not get sand in them. "Why didn't you come back last night?" I said.

"The oceans. The one out here and the one behind the porthole."

"What?"

"Come on," she said, standing up and taking my hand.

"Donna, I have to get to work."

She nodded. "You keep saying that. Fuck work. This is important."

"Can't we talk about it later?"

She stopped and turned to look at me.

"Can you come home early?" she said.

"I'll try, okay?"

She nodded.

I worked later than usual that night and I figured she was so angry that she had gone to bed, which was fine with me, but when I went into the bathroom I found her on her hands and knees, sopping up water with a sponge.

The mirror was leaking, water seeping through the bottom, between the teak and the brass.

"I don't understand why you haven't noticed," she said. She sat cross-legged on the floor, her hands wringing the sponge compulsively, leaving a water stain on the thigh of her jeans. Small tears rolled down her cheeks, echoing the drops from the mirror. "At first I hoped you wouldn't see it, then I couldn't understand why you didn't."

"How can a mirror leak?"

She shook her head. "I don't know. I don't know." She buried her face in her hands and cried. The sponge rolled off her lap and onto the floor. I knelt down beside her and put my arm across her shoulder, careful not to put my knee in the puddle.

"Look, it's probably nothing. Water's leaking somewhere and it's catching on the inside of the porthole. There's room in back for that."

She nodded and sniffed. "But it's salty."

"What?" I reached up, touched a drop, and brought it carefully to my mouth.

"Plaster dust," I told her.

"You think so?"

"Sure," I lied, not knowing what I thought.

Donna finished mopping up while I watched the beads of water form at the bottom of the mirror. I began fumbling with the latch.

"Don't," Donna shouted when she looked up. My hands jumped from the mirror. I was more nervous than I thought. "Don't open it."

"Why not?"

She stood slowly and stared at me. Her eyes were dry and clear now. "I don't know. I just don't think it would be a good idea, that's all."

"Don't you want to know where the water is coming from?"

She nodded. "Take it off the wall. Don't open it, just take it off the wall." Her voice was tightly controlled.

Shaking my head at this new whim, I turned to the mirror and lifted. It did not move.

"Did you nail it in?"

"No, we just hung it on two hooks, remember?"

"I meant after that, when I wasn't here." I was getting annoyed at her. I yanked again, harder, but nothing happened. The hooks were near the top; the bottom and sides should have levered up. Leaning into the wall I tried to see what was holding it. The wall and mirror were seamless, as if though a complex series of molecule shifts, the plaster, paint and teakwood had combined into a single composite element. As I watched, the dripping increased to a trickle.

I raced through the apartment gathering tools. Back in the bathroom I put a screwdriver where I expected a seam to be and slammed it with a hammer. Nothing happened. I moved the screwdriver out a little and struck again. For an inch and a half around the porthole mirror the plaster was indestructible. Beyond that it was plain plaster again, shattering into dust and chunks. Donna stood silently the whole time, winching each time I punched another hole in her wall. Then she knelt down, licked her finger, touched the dust, and brought the white powder to her tongue.

"It's not salty," she said. I did not answer.

We stood together, watching the water drip and puddle at our feet. Donna bent down again, took her sponge and began mopping.

"Maybe it would be simpler just to open it up," I suggested.

"No."

There was no room for argument. I was relieved. I was not sure I wanted to argue.

"We can dig though the wall from behind and get it loose," she said.

For a moment it seemed like a good idea. Then I shook my head. "It's an outside wall. Do you want to crawl out the little window with a pickaxe while I hold your feet or shall we do it the other way around? It's only four stories down if I drop you." She giggled nervously. The trickling increased. Her giggle dissolved into a sob.

"Look, it's probably just a pipe back there leaking."

"Salt water?" Her tone was sarcastic. "Besides, you just said it's an outside wall. They don't run pipes through outside walls." Before I could think of another explanation, she continued, "and leaking water doesn't make plaster harder. Even I know that."

"Do you want to tell the building manager?"

"What do I tell him? That behind my mirror there's a god-damn ocean trying to get into my apartment and I want him to do something about it? Come on, be realistic. You've heard it, I know you have, even if you don't want to admit it. There were waves back there. Just like the waves down on the beach. It's my ocean in there. I dreamed it and wished for it and now it's here. My own private ocean."

"But the sound stopped," I said.

"Only when the ocean covered the back of the porthole."

Crying now, she pushed past me and headed for the kitchen. I began to follow, then the stupidity of what she said reached me. She was being irrational; we both were. There were no waves behind the mirror. It was impossible. The noises had ended weeks before and whatever they were, they were not waves. It was wind scraping the side of the building. It was the swish of a tree branch. It was a complex echo from the beach two and a half blocks away. Yet here we were, two people believing there was water behind a porthole mirror. We were sharing a delusion we had talked ourselves and each other into.

I held my hand against the mirror. There was no push from behind it, no tidal wave forcing its way in. I sighed with relief and called to Donna.

In the doorway, she shrieked, "Are you out of your mind? Don't."

I was suddenly afraid to pull open the porthole. I held the latch as tightly as I could. I don't think Donna could see I hadn't unlocked it when her hand swatted mine away. The latch snapped and the porthole swung open slamming into the wall. Following it came a torrent of water, smashing into the room with the force of a fire hose, pounding into the opposite wall and pouring onto the floor. I tried to push it closed again but there was too much pressure.

Donna and I faced each other across a hideous horizontal fountain. Water was already seeping into my socks. The noise was deafening. I ducked under the water.

"Come on," I shouted, grabbing for Donna's hand. She pulled it away.

"I'm going to try closing it."

"You can't." I grabbed again, but she was under the water, splashing up to her shins, both hands now pushing against the front of the mirror, water cascading off of it.

"We can't just leave it."

"Listen, you try. I'll get help. Then meet me downstairs in half an hour."

"Why?"

"We've got to get out of here," I shouted. "Maybe California."

"Okay,"

I ran out. The apartment had been turned into a shallow wading pool already, water covering the foyer, kitchen and living room. The bedroom rug was soaked on one end. Out the front door was another large puddle. People were opening their doors as I ran down the steps. I thought it was not smart for Donna to stay, but it was her decision.

It was her porthole, after all.

"Pipe broke," I shouted. "I'm going to get a plumber."

Outside, I told a cop what was really going on. He wanted me to go back up with him, but I told him I was going to get a wrench to shut the water off in the basement. I think the only reason he went in was to humor me. I kept running, first down to Surf Avenue, then east toward Brighton Beach, back to my apartment. I had some dry clothes there and some camping equipment I might need. My breathing was heavy and my chest began to hurt when I passed the aquarium. I walked the last quarter of a mile.

From my apartment, I dialed Donna's number. There was no answer. I packed a few things, mostly jeans and work shirts and my ski parka and hiking boots. I did not have fuel for the portable camping stove, but I figured I could buy it on the way. I guessed I had a couple of days at least before the stores ran out.

I tried to drive back to Donna's apartment, but Surf Avenue had already been closed. There was a cop turning all the cars back. I pulled over and got out to find out what was going on.

"Water main break," she said. "Street collapsed." I nodded and walked back to my car.

Neptune Avenue brought me two blocks closer to the apartment, but there was a cop there too. I drove slowly around the periphery, looking for Donna. The police were still letting walkers through, but I didn't want to leave the car. What if someone panicked and stole it? How would Donna and I get away?

She had probably left by now anyway. I saw a lot of people leaving. I headed for the Belt Parkway and the Verrazano Bridge. I wanted to get through Staten Island and into central New Jersey before midnight, before the rush. I would probably link up with Donna later, headed west. California, here we come.

The next morning I heard a news story on the radio that the building had collapsed due to water damage caused by a major water main break. There were no reported injuries because the building had been abandoned three years ago, the report said.

They also reported that fifteen people had drowned in Prospect Park lake when the paddleboats they were riding in had a freak accident. The reporter sounded like he did not believe the story, but that's because he was in Manhattan. The water did not reach Manhattan until the next day.

I took my time now, driving a few hours a day, buying small stores of supplies and putting it on my Visa card. In Cleveland, I got a hotel room and switched to CNN. The building was a pile of waterlogged rubble, and I hoped that in collapsing it had closed the hole. But the report was that a long-buried underground stream in Brooklyn had suddenly surfaced in Coney Island. The Army Corps of Engineers was building a levee and a small dam on the north side of the Belt Parkway. A few thousand people were listed as dead or missing. From a boat, they showed a picture of the old Parachute Jump ride. Half of it was underwater already. I wondered if Donna was a good swimmer. There are lakes in Canada, and she loved the ocean. It's just too bad we got split up.

That was three months ago. They call it Lake Jersey now, a name that began as a joke, before they believed the water would reach New Jersey. Actually, it reached Allentown in just over five weeks. It will be a while before it gets over the Alleghenies. The most popular theory is that the ice caps are melting because of the greenhouse effect.

In Colorado, where I ended up, things stayed pretty much the same. We are pretty high up, as everyone knows.

But I read the other day that the tides were unusually high in Portugal and that a storm had cut all links to the Azores. I wonder how many people know what's really going on?

I am hoping that soon the water will reach a point of stasis. A lot of water had already poured though the porthole; it's only a matter of time before sea level on this side is the same as sea level on the other side.

I've called the number in Brooklyn, but nothing happens. It's as if there's nothing connected at the other end. I've called her father in Alberta twice. The first time he said he said he hadn't heard from her; the second time I could tell just from the way her mother answered the telephone that they were very worried, so I didn't say anything. My guess is she headed straight to California to look for me. I should write to her soon, while the Postal Service is still operating, let her know I'm all right. Maybe I'll contact the local art students league in Santa Monica or something.

I wish she was here with me, though. She was always good with plants, and my tomatoes are not doing very well. Too much moisture, I think.

# Just Don't Block the View...
## Michael Jahn

Excerpted from *City of God*, St. Martin's Press, 1992

AVIGNON FELT A GREAT SURGE OF ADRENALIN when news came over the police radio that a ghastly hostage scene, one with much potential for glorious and photogenic bloodshed, was shaping up in Coney Island. The surge started in the back of his head and travelled down his spine to his loins, where it nestled comfortably next to the other force that drove his life.

Newark Airport had been a bust. The crippled 747 inbound from Shannon with 347 passengers on board and two dead engines failed to live up to its potential for carnage. The plane made it onto the runway not only intact, but with no visible damage. And the passengers debarked unruffled, with the exception of one old lady who had to be given oxygen and hauled off in a wheelchair. The footage he shot wouldn't make the 6 o'clock news on the *local* stations, let alone the networks.

But a hostage scene in the world's most famous laughing junkyard, complete with SWAT teams and horrified, weeping neighbors! That was the stuff of which Academy Awards were made.

Avignon dropped the gearshift down into third and put the pedal to the metal. The 420-horsepower engine roared, shoving the grand old Chevy forward around the rim of the City of New York. Avignon blew by a Cadillac and half a dozen Japanese cars, the twin chrome exhausts smoking the asphalt of the Belt Parkway. Avignon swept round the bend through the Narrows, the maw of America. A strait of perilous water at the mouth of New York Harbor, it sucked in the world's refuse and spat it backwards across the land. Brooklyn was the gatekeeper, and home to the most recent arrivals, some of whom tarried on their way to discover America to visit Coney Island. One of *them* had apparently decided to turn his wife into a Swanson's Ethnic Entree.

Avignon caught the southbound ramp onto Cropsey Avenue and, soon after, raced west on Surf Avenue past a junkyard of garish smiles and blaring signs, many with towering exclamation points made of rusted iron and broken glass. At the Thunderbolt!, the dot beneath the dagger was home to a pair of pigeons grown fat from eating the scraps that spilled from Nathan's dumpsters.

The birds were among the few signs of life. The once-thriving roller coaster was another skeleton where once New Yorkers played by the boardwalk. The one-time attraction was small compared to the Cyclone; less a Thunderbolt! than a backfire from a Model T. It rose four or five stories in each of its three apexes, sinewing down to twin valleys where the oxidated rails and worm-eaten scaffolding grazed the tips of a waving field of waist-high goldenrod. At its closest approach to the boardwalk, the rails reached skyward and made an abrupt turn directly over a two-story souvenir shack that history had turned into a boarded-up caretaker's cottage. Therein hung the tale that Avignon sensed was the photogenic catastrophe to beat all; the one to ensure his place in history as America's foremost video documentarist.

The decrepit fun ride was in a panic over a crackpot with a shotgun who was holding hostage his common-law wife. She had practiced indiscretion with a local grocer, and would be shot dead for it if the police didn't go away. Avignon had heard that line a million times: "If you don't go away I'll kill her," they said. Avignon wondered what would the man do if the police did go away. Kiss her, make up, and give her a Whitman's Sampler? Take her and mom to Sunday Mass at Our Lady of the Sodden Death and then to Friendly's for a butterscotch sundae? And what of Coney Island, which had seen frequent murderous acts during the current century? "Indian burial ground," Avignon mused, wielding an old theory of his that many sites within the city were built on sacred Indian burial grounds and forever jinxed.

Avignon pulled up behind a line of police cars and was immediately hemmed in by three others. The block of West 16th Street from Surf Avenue to the boardwalk had come to resemble a blue-and-white parking lot, one brightened by dozens of flashing red lights and the crackle of radios. The brown Emergency Services SWAT van stood in the midst of it all, alongside a nine-foot chain-link fence topped with barbed wire that served as flypaper for bits of black plastic garbage bag borne there by the wind and flapped to shreds. Coney Island pirate flags. The caretaker's cottage was walled in part by corrugated steel and part by hastily tacked up tarpaper. The windows on the ground floor were covered with plywood. A whitewashed wooden door was partly obscured by a green 1979 Plymouth that tilted drunkenly backwards onto a flat tire.

From the lone second-story window, a fat bald man, black chest hair sprouting from between the buttons of an outgrown shirt, held a shotgun and yelled threats. A hostage-situation detective, trained to talk sense into lunatics bearing lethal weapons—a type of cop that always reminded Avignon of a priest—was talking calm and reassurance through a megaphone while hiding behind the van.

Avignon slid onto the pavement on the opposite side of his car from the house. He plucked the Ikegami from the back seat, slipped in a fresh cartridge of crystal black videotape, then set the videocamera on his shoulder. Standing tall, he tried out the focus on a uniformed patrolman who duck-walked over, carefully staying out of the line-of-fire.

"Who are you?" the cop asked.

"Press," Avignon said, without taking his attention from the eyepiece.

"Prove it."

Avignon flipped his yellow plastic police badge out of his jacket pocket. The young officer squinted at the badge, still afraid to stand up. "Never heard of Crystal Black News," he said.

Avignon focused his lens on the man's name tag, then said, "That's okay, Officer Repetti, I never heard of you either."

The young officer bristled, copped an especially nasty Brooklyn attitude, and was about to risk standing up, the better to scream at the wise guy, when a tall man, greying at the temples and possessed of a commanding air, strolled by. "Leave him alone, officer," he said.

"Yes sir, Captain," Repetti said quickly, and scurried off. Avignon grunted in gratitude and closed the car door.

"I'll give you twenty for it," the man said, patting the convertible top of Avignon's beloved 1957 Chevy.

"I told you last week I'm not selling. Who's the guy with the shotgun?"

"Some guinea whose wife cheated on him. Twenty-five."

"You're a dreamer. Is the guy serious?"

A shotgun burst roared and a patrol car ten yards down the block was peppered with holes. The cops hiding behind it hit the pavement.

"He's serious," the captain said, like Avignon a combat veteran and unfazed. "Twenty-five is my last offer. Better take it, Mike. You might not live till noon."

Avignon said, "He's a mackerel-snapper like you whose god won't let him commit suicide. He wants you to shoot him so he can ride off to the promised land with a clear conscience."

"Sell me the car and I'll shoot him."

From all around them came the sound of guns being cocked.

Avignon focused the Ikegami on the second-story window, then said "He's got his gun set with the choke wide open. It we were a bit further away we could hide behind a garbage bag, the pellets are spreading so wide." Avignon started for the ramp up to the boardwalk, which he guessed offered a good vantage point for the unfolding carnage.

"Hey Mike," the captain yelled. "Stand in the middle of the boardwalk and wave your arms. Let's see how good the bastard's aim is."

"I love you too, Donovan," Avignon yelled back.

Two patrol cars to the north, seven or eight sergeants and a lieutenant were caught up in a hasty conference. Avignon wondered just when the decision-by-committee mentality hit the police department. To his admittedly old-fashioned way of thinking, there were only two choices to be made when being shot at—shoot back or run away.

Sirens heralded the arrival of more decision-makers, probably a few division commanders and the borough chief. All of Avignon's old friends in the department couldn't protect him from the wrath of the Brooklyn Borough Chief, who was still pissed off trying to figure out how Avignon snuck a videocamera inside Federal District Court for the arraignment of the deputy mayor.

The boardwalk planks swelled in the August heat but still allowed Avignon to glimpse twenty feet down to the plastic bottles, bleached food wrappers, and shrivelled condoms below. A sulking grey oil tanker crept in from the Atlantic but the sea was otherwise barren. The boardwalk itself was a riot of portablecarbon fiber barricades that the police department had bought on the promise they were bulletproof. Junior officers had hauled them up for their betters to hide behind and, while they and a few stray civilians were doing just that, no one looked entirely convinced of the wisdom of the investment.

Avignon ducked behind one nonetheless, and there found a Greek and his wife shifting their weights nervously, still suffering the shock of becoming extras in a television drama. Police sharpshooters behind the other barriers aimed high-powered rifles at the miscreant's window. Feeling a new batch of adrenalin flush through his system, Avignon aimed the Ikegami. A Greek accent sprouted from a barrel chest. "That bum, I always knew he was nuts," said an unshaven man in loose-fitting cotton pants and a sleeveless undershirt from which sprouted even more black hair.

Avignon glanced at the fellow. "How long have you known him, Mr....?"

"George Nikolatos," the man replied, proudly spelling his name. "I known him since he moved in three years ago. The guy's a nut. Crazy, you know? I always said he was gonna kill somebody some day."

Avignon grinned. It was refreshing to find a lunatic's acquaintance who could see it coming. So often they said, "I can't believe he slaughtered his whole family. He loved kids and dogs and was good to his missus and mom. Every Sunday he took her to Our Lady of the Sodden Death and then to Friendly's."

"What's his name and what's he do?"

Nikolatos told Avignon that the man was named Thomas Rotundi and that he had, for the years since the Thunderbolt! closed, eked out a living as night watchman and caretaker, charged with defending the structure against the city's ubiquitous thrill-vandals.

"No wonder he's nuts," Avignon said. "Having to work and sleep in a tin shack beneath rusting roller coaster rails." Avignon thought, but not out loud, of the ghosts of the long-ago patrons howling gleefully over Rotundi's barren marital bed, night after night after sleepless night.

"A couple months ago he came outta the house with his shotgun and blew the shit out of the garbage can."

"Did he say why? Didn't he like garbage?"

The Greek looked at Avignon as if he were the crazy one. Avignon picked up the gaffe, and said, "Right. You decided not to ask."

"No kidding. What channel are you with? You are TV, right?"

"I shoot for whoever has money. Today's it's ABC—Channel 7. Did Rotundi do anything else crazy?"

"A lot of yelling. I think he beat up his missus. She never came out of the house."

Avignon peered through the lens at ground zero. He could see almost directly into Rotundi's bedroom. The man had his wife by the back of the neck and was holding the shotgun to her head, daring the police to come and get him. She was impassive, almost limp, nearly dead already or resigned to death like a rabbit in the jaws of a wolf.

Through the eyepiece Avignon could see far enough into the room to make out a painting on the far wall, but not details of it. Rotundi's shirt was monogrammed on the pocket, and he was sweating. It was uncommonly hot, even for August, the predicted greenhouse-effect warming of the earth having arrived early. This was the fifth straight sweltering summer in New York City, and already shaky city nerves were jangling especially loud. Rotundi came home from his rounds of Coney Island to find it was a hundred and forty in the corrugated tin house, and there was also the cuckolding wife. The laughing ghosts on the rails over his head were unusually amused as his wits abandoned him.

Avignon rested the camera on the boardwalk, just in time to notice that Nikolatos had opened a vinyl bag to produce a spanking-new Magnavox home videocamera, one made with as many fancy displays and readouts as possible. "How do you like this?" the Greek asked, proudly displaying the machine. "My wife got it for me for Christmas. It cost her a thousand dollars. It takes good pictures."

Avignon agreed, in his fashion. "It's a pretty camera, and made by Matsushita, one of the best in Japan."

"Japan? Come on, this is American...got an American name: Magnavox."

"Unh...sure, my mistake."

Nikolatos indicated Avignon's Ikegami, which was burnished black, scratched and dented from hard service, and relatively uncluttered-looking. "How much you pay for that?"

"Fifty," Avignon said, a bit uncomfortably.

"Fifty what?"

"Fifty thousand."

The Greek's shoulders dropped. Avignon had upstaged him, and immediately felt regret. He said, "Hey, this is how I make my living. What do you do?"

"I'm a butcher."

"I bet your knives cost a lot more than mine."

Nikolatos smiled. "I got a carving knife that cost me three hundred."

"See? I got a whole set from Macy's for thirty bucks."

The Greek laughed and clapped Avignon on the shoulder. Before an I-can-get-knives-for-you-wholesale offer could be tendered, Avignon picked up the Ikegami and began shooting the general commotion: the cops, the cars with the red lights, the Brooklyn Borough Chief off safely to one side, giving a statement to a small herd of newspapermen. Avignon's camera caught Nikolatos repeating his assessment of Rotundi.

Then Nikolatos tried to shoot some footage with his toy camera, but Avignon shooed him back safely behind the barricade. "It's going to start happening soon," he said. "I can tell."

"How?"

"I've been doing this for twenty-five years. It's second nature. There's a disturbance in the air that I can feel. Especially in Coney Island, where the air was disturbed to begin with."

The Greek offered a rather suspicious look and let Avignon go about his business. But indeed, after only a few minutes, the mood changed subtly. There was something in the air. Avignon had been shooting film and videotape since he was twenty-one and was widely considered the best in New York. He was certainly the boldest, having turned a talent for sniffing out what he called "photogenic catastrophes" into a small empire. He always was in the right place at the right time; could, as he boasted, feel the air tense up, as if huge, invisible hands had grabbed it like a cheap pair of panty hose and stretched it tight.

He focused once again on Rotundi's bedroom. The man and woman had pulled back inside, and their shadows could vaguely be seen on the wall. Without them blocking the view, Avignon saw the details of the painting. It was the dime-store variety picture of the Virgin Mary, paint on black velvet, her arms outstretched to the heavens, her eyes slightly raised.

"Terrific," Avignon said to himself, clenching shut his eyes and recalling his childhood claim on telepathy. Once again that child, he spoke to Rotundi: "Just don't block the view of the Virgin when you come to the window to get your head blown off."

Avignon hadn't been talking entirely to himself, as he had thought.

"What?" Nikolatos asked.

"I'm just lining up the shot. Like you might guess where to cut a hunk of beef."

"Guessing has nothing to do with it."

"My point exactly."

That seemed reasonable to the Greek, who took a quick look around the corner of the barricade before pulling back.

Avignon saw Emergency Services cops in flak jackets moving up behind Rotundi's house. That was it; it was they who were stretching the air. "It's happening," Avignon said, and began taping.

There was motion in the bedroom. A shadow moved erratically across and away from the Virgin Mary.

A police bullhorn broke the silence. Rotundi was warned of his last chance.

"Ten seconds," Avignon said.

He recalled his high school days, when he first took photos of basketball games. He always knew when the guy was going to make a jump shot. He always pressed the shutter at the height of the action, when the air was stretched as tight as it would go. The talent had come to make him rich and famous.

Avignon sucked in his breath. There came a woman's scream and a shotgun blast. Several of the younger policemen dived for cover, and walkie-talkies crackled with urgent orders.

"Now," Avignon said.

There was another moving shadow, and Rotundi burst into the camera's frame and became captured for all time on crystal black videotape, the very best kind used exclusively by the very best.

The man fired two bursts at the assembled on the boardwalk. Then were was a volley of return fire from the police. Rotundi was cut nearly in half by a dozen bullets. The body jerked backwards, then tumbled forwards and was caught, bent, over the windowsill, half outside. The shotgun hung from his lifeless fingers for a second, then dropped leadenly to the ground.

Avignon's breath caught in his throat; all of a sudden the wife hurled herself at the window, crying hysterically, clutching at her husband's bloody corpse. She tried to yank it back into the room and, that failing, tossed her hands up toward an unfeeling god and let out a wail.

Avignon watched and the camera whirled. There she was, immortalized, standing over the remains of her husband, wailing with the painting of the Virgin Mary framed between her uplifted arms.

"Academy Award," Avignon gasped.

# A Coney Island of the Mind
*Maureen F. McHugh*

REALITY PARLOR.

He pays his money and goes back to the cubicle with the treadmill and pulls on the waldos, puts on the heavy eyeless, earless helmet. He grabs for the handlebars suspended before him, blind in the helmet that smells intimately of someone else's hair.

Now he can see. Not the handlebars hung from the ceiling on a tape-wrapped cable, not the treadmill. He is the cat with future feet. He sees a schematic of a room; all the lines of the room are in pink neon on velvet black, and in his ears instead of the seasound of the helmet he hears the sound of open space. A room sounds different than a helmet even when there's nothing to hear.

A keyboards appears, or rather a line drawing of a keyboard with all the letters on the keys glowing neon blue. Over it in neon-blue letters is the message, "Please type in your user ID."

"Cobalt," he types, letting go of the handlebars. The waldos give him the sensation of hitting keys, give him feedback. His password is nagasaki.

A neon pink door draws itself in the velvet wall in front of him. The keyboard disappears and the handlbars appear in pink neon schematic until he grabs them. Then they disappear from sight, but he can still feel them, safe in his gloved hands. He starts forward [the treadmill lurches a bit under his blind feet but it always does that at first so he is accustomed to it, doesn't really think about it, just kind of expects it and forgets about it] through the door which opens up ahead of him, pulling apart like elevator doors into the party.

The party isn't a schematic, the party looks real. The party is a big space full of people dressed all ways—boys with big hair and girls with latex skulls and NPC in evening gowns and tuxes—and as he comes out of the elevator he looks to the right, to the mirrors and sees himself, sees Cobalt, sees a Tom Sawyer in the twenty-first century, a flagboy in a bluesilk jacket and thigh-high boots with a knot of burgundy cords at the hips. All angles in the face, smooth face like a razor, a face he had custom-configured in hours of bought-time at the reality parlor, not playing the reality streets, not even looking, just working at his own look. Cobalt eyes like lasers, and blue-steel braids for hair.

Edgelook, whatta-look, hot damn.

Not what he looks like at all in the mundane world of Cincinnati, Ohio, but he isn't in Cincinnati, ho, flagboy, he's not in Kansas any more, he is at *the party*. Here he is, a serious dog, a democratic dog, but he doesn't think he'll spend a lot of time at the party today, looking around he doesn't see anyone he knows. Not that that means they aren't there, because anybody can look like anything, but if they don't have a handle he recognizes and they don't go calling out to Cobalt then they don't want to be the people he knows, right? and anyway, this afternoon the partyroom is full of off-the-racks, look-like-your-favorite-movie-star or take-a-basic-template-what-color-are-your-eyes-your-hair-look-like-a-manikin which he can't abide because he's looking for people with style so he angles over towards the far wall [his real feet, his mundane feet in their grass-stained sneakers that he wears when he mows the lawn just keep heading straight on the treadmill, if he angles he'll step off the treadmill, but he turns the handlebars to the left and he's done it so long he doesn't get confused by his feet saying one direction and the handlebars telling him another] to the far wall, full of blank doorways and he stops to read the menu.

It's better now that he's turned eighteen, more choices. Games and Adventures, Simulations, Tanks and Airplanes and Spaceships—but he's not really interested in a lot of that because he's on a treadmill, not sitting down, so back to Games and Adventures, Places To Go and Things To Do, where he is likely to find some people he knows, someone to hang out with; Quixote and Bushman and Taipei.

"Any messages?" he asks out loud.

Soft chime that can be heard over the whole room of the party (except that no one else does.) No messages. Nobody in the swim? Then he'll look for a place where maybe he'll meet serious dogs. He almost selects Chinatown but changes his mind and [left hand lets go of the handlebars and reaches out] pushes the button for Coney Island.

[Feedback through the waldo, it feels like pushing something.]

A line of electricity forms at the top of the door, a forcefield, an edge of static that rolls down like a window shade only draws down an opening on a place.

Black night on the boardwalk with the Ferris Wheel and the parachute drop all decked out in colored lights off in the distance. Cobalt steps through the door and his feet thump the hollow wood of the boradwalk. The booths spill bright white and yellow light onto the boards. He can hear the ocean. A guy is selling hot dogs. Coney fucking Island.

So he walks down the boardwalk, checking out the crowd, checking out how much is just program—the sailor and his girl at the Toss The Ring who are always at the Toss The Ring every time he comes—and how much is real people. It's a quiet night on the boardwalk.

Maybe he should go back to the party, check out Chinatown. Hey, he's here, maybe he'll just dogtrot on down the boardwalk, out towards the rides, see if there's someone. Then he'll go back to Chinatown.

Moving along the boardwalk, past the cotton candy, past the tattoo parlor,past the place where the counter is a two-tone Cadillac, dog gone, dog going, into a dog eat dog world.

And the queens (who are mostly black and tall and female and camp, that being the current fashion in queens) are calling "Hey sweetcakes," "Hey, be my blueboy," "Are you hotwired, babyface?" "Are you wired for sound?" Which he's not because he rents time in a fucking public reality parlor (no pun intended) where they aren't going to supply equipment to wire your crotch.

But it's all just noise, white noise, background hiss, the sound of Coney Island and not what he's looking for anyway although who's to say what he'd be looking for if he had the option? But he doesn't, so he isn't, he's looking for his mates, his team, his dogpack. He's checking under the boardwalk behind the Chinese Food place, and watching the mustangs crawl up the street because Quixote like simulations, likes to drive fast cars in crazy places. Watching for spies because Taipei likes adventure games where he fights off attackers, watches for gang members because they all like to play Warriors and Coney Island is where it starts, where they catch the subway to the cemetery in the Bronx.

But the streets are all full of programming, of nonplayer characters, and kids without style, which is to say that this night Coney Island is empty.

So he's thinking that he'll check one more place, maybe take in a movie, or call up the airlock and go on to Chinatown and he stops where he can see the ocean and looks for a moment, the stone dark ocean rolling and making that sound, hypnotizing him and he likes it because there isn't much ocean in Cincinatti, hell, there isn't even much sin in Cincinatti.

She leans next to him with a star hanging off her ear, one lone star in the smoke nebula of her shadow hair, no off-the-rack handle but a costume full of style, like himself, like the dogpack, this woman has taken some time. "Hey blueboy," she says.

"Hey yourself," he says and imagines she smells like perfume, smells like ash. She has full breasts and brown skin in the yellow light. She has yellow snake eyes, not like dice like rattlesnakes and hair that doesn't act like real hair at all but fills some indefinite space, swallows light, absorbs light, no reflections. Soft looking. Nice touch, that. She's a chimera, she's not content to take a strictly human template, she's diddled the programming.

He's a lucky dog.

They make noises in the night, what's your name, Cobalt what's yours? (Rattlesnake, he wonders, or cobra, coral snake, black racer, asp, gila monster,his mind all in a rush before she answers—)

Lamia.

Which isn't what he expected at all and doesn't mean a thing except it sounds liquid. He wishes he had more access, he wishes he had preprogrammed something, an ashen rose maybe, to pull out of the air and give to her, but all he has are things that are useful in adventure games; a smoke bomb, a rope, a bottle that can be broken and used like a knife.

"That's pretty," he says.

She reaches out and takes his hand. And sighs happily.

The ocean rolls in.

"Squeeze," she says in a throaty whisper.

For a moment he doesn't understand but then he squeezes her hand and she half-closes her eyes. "Flagboy," she says, "I think I like you,."

"Want to walk on the beach?" he asks.

She shrugs and kneads his fingers, he can feel her hand, all the bones of it and her long fingers, and she can feel his because of the waldos. He pulls her towards the steps and she gives a throaty, gaspy laugh.

She's wearing high heels, spikes with toes like cloven hooves—except that her feet don't look human. Her smoky hair has horns, then it's a halo, a madonna veil, all smoke. She follows him in a clatter across the hollow boards and down the steps into the sand. Their footsteps become silent [it never feels any different, because his feet are still on the treadmill, and his right hand is still on the handlebars, but his left holds the air and the waldos mimic the pressure of her hand.]

"Not so tight," she says, and he loosens his grip on her hand.

Eyes and hands, eyes and ears and hands. How real is real?

The light from the star in her hair falls on her bare shoulders, on her collar bones. Her clothing has no reason to stay covering her breasts but it does. She wouldn't feel it if her touched her breasts, not unless she's wearing a hotsuit. Could she be wearing a hotsuit, have her whole body wired for touch? Does she have a place at home, a treadmill, the whole bit? Spoiled Fifth Avenue girl? LA girl? Maybe she's forty years old, he doesn't know. Maybe she's ugly.

Interesting thought, that. He looks at her smoky hair and her skin and the hollow leading into her heart-shaped top and squeezes her hand and she sighs. Huuuhhh.

And he sighs too. Maybe she's ugly, or fat, or old. Maybe she is blind, or deformed. Maybe she is married. Wild thought that this beautiful girl can be anything.

His heart is pounding. She stops and they are facing each other, holding hands. If they kissed, there would be nothing but air. Strange to feel her through his palm and fingers, the waldos giving him all the feelings of her hand, and knowing that he could pass his arm through her. She is nothing but light. If he thinks about it he can feel the weight of the helmet on his head.

And her hand. All the bones and tendons and ligaments, the elastic play of her muscle. He finds her fingers, presses them one-by-one. She is watching his with slit-pupiled snake eyes gone from amber to green, although he can't remember when that happened. The ocean roars behind them.

He laces his fingers through hers. "Where are you?" he asks, althouigh it's rude to ask people that.

"On the boardwalk," she says, her voice coming out in a breath. She is watching him, lazily intent, and he is playing with her hand. She closes her eyes and catches her lip in her teeth. Her face is so strange.

"Don't stop," she whispers and he doesn't know what she is talking about and then he realizes it is her hand, her hand in his blue gloved one. Her face is almost empty of expression, but small things seem to be happening in it independent of anything that is in his face.

"Squeeze," she says again.

Confused, he does, and feels her squeezing rhythmically back, pulsing little squeezes, and he realizes in horror just—

[She's hotwired her hand.]

—as she comes. Eyes shut, smoky hair rising in horns, she gasps a little. He jerks his hand away, but she is standing there oblivious, and it's too late anyway.

[You take a hot suit and rewire the crotch so the system thinks it's a hand, then any time someone touches your hand...]

He is embarrassed, angry, shocked. He doesn't know if he should just go or not.

[His fingers squeezing her and he didn't know.]

"Blueboy," she says, and sits down on the sand. "Oh Christ, blueboy."

He will go, and he does [turning the handlebars; feet, as always, straight on the treadmill] and starts back for the steps.

"Cone one," she says, "what's so awful about it?"

"You didn't tell me," he says, all indignation.

"Prissy little virgin," she says, and laughs behind him.

"Airlock," he says, which is a system command, a gateway back to the party. The line of static starts at the height of a door, and the forcefield rolls down like a window shade.

"Huff on out of here," she says. "Righteous little bitch. Are you a girl?"

"What!?" he says.

Which makes her laugh. [Somewhere in Cincinatti his cheeks are burning.]

"I'm glad," she said, "because I'm not into girls. I just like wearing girl bodies because I like you righteous boys, you sweet straight boys."

He starts to step into the party and stops. "What?" he says.

"Draws you all like moths to a flame," she says. Or he says, or it said.

His first swift thought is that he'll have to change his look, never look like this again, abandon Cobalt, be something else.

She laughs that ashen laugh. "Go on home, blue boy."

And he does, steps back into the party, leaves Coney Island behind. The party, neutral ground, where he shakes his head, dog shaking water off his coat. He blinks in the lights of the party. Thinks of going home, going back to Cincinnatti, to thinking about Ohio State in the fall.

Trying not to think about feet like hooves, high heels.

What a frigging nut case!

Bad luck, Quixote is waving across the space. Cobalt doesn't know, just wants to go home.

"Where you been," Quixote says, "you're looking democratic."

Shrugs. What's he going to say, I met this girl—I met this girl and her hand...he starts to smile, what a dog story. Quixote is going to be green.

"You won't believe what happened to me in Coney Island," Cobalt says.

He doesn't have top tell everything.

"No way!" Quixote says.

It's a dog eat dog world, sometimes.

—*for Bob Yeager*

# Beachcomber

## *Mike Resnick*

Arlo didn't look much like a man. (Not all robots do, you know.) The problem was that he didn't act all that much like a robot.

The fact of the matter is that one day, right in the middle of work, he decided to pack it in. Just got up, walked out the door, and kept on going. *Some*body must have seen him; it's pretty hard to hide nine hundred pounds of moving parts. But evidently nobody knew it was Arlo. After all, he hadn't left his desk since the day they'd activated him twelve years ago.

So the Company got in touch with me, which is a euphemistic way of saying that they woke me in the middle of the night, gave me three minutes to get dressed, and rushed me to the office. I can't really say that I blame them: when you need a scapegoat, the Chief of Security is a pretty handy guy to have around.

Anyway, it was panic time. It seems that no robot ever ran away before. And Arlo wasn't just any robot: he was a twelve million dollar item, with just about every feature a machine could have short of white-walled tires. And I wasn't even certain about the tires; he sure dropped out of sight fast enough.

So, after groveling a little and making all kinds of optimistic promises to the Board, I started doing a little checking up on Arlo. I went to his designer, and his department head, and even spoke to some of his co-workers, both humans and robot.

And it turned out that what Arlo did was sell tickets. That didn't sound like twelve million dollars' worth of robot to me, but I was soon shown the error of my ways. Arlo was a travel agent supreme. He booked tours of the Solar System, got his people into and out of luxury hotels on Ganymede and Titan and the Moon, scheduled their weight and their time to the nearest gram and nearest second.

It still didn't sound that impressive. Computers were doing stuff like that long before robots ever crawled out of the pages of pulp magazines and into our lives.

"True," said his department head. "But Arlo was a robot with a difference. Ho booked more tours and arranged more complicated logistical scheduling than any other ten robots put together."

"More complex thinking gear?" I asked.

"Well, that too," was the answer. "But we did a little something else with Arlo that had never been done before."

"Ands what was that?"

"We programmed him for enthusiasm."

"That's something special?" I asked.

"Absolutely. When Arlo spoke about the beauties of Callisto, or the fantastic light refraction images on Venus, he did so with a conviction that was so intense as to be almost tangible. Even his voice reflected his enthusiasm. He was one of those rare robots who was capable of modular inflection, rather than the dull, mechanistic monotone so many of them possess. He literally loved those desolate worlds, and his record will show that his attitude was infectious."

I thought about that for a minute. "So you're telling me that you've created a robot whose entire motivation had been to send people out to sample all those worlds, and he's been crated up in an office twenty-four hours a day since the second you plugged him in?"

"That's correct."

"Did it ever occur to you that maybe he wanted to see some of these sights himself?"

"It's entirely possible that he did, but leaving his post would be contrary to orders."

"Yeah," I said. "Well, sometimes a little enthusiasm can go a long way."

He denied it vigorously, and I spent just enough time in his office to mollify him. Then I left and got down to work. I checked every outgoing space flight, and had some of the Company's field reps hit the more luxurious vacation spas. He wasn't there.

So I tried a little closer to home: Monte Carlo, New Vegas, Alpine City. No luck. I even tried a couple of local theaters that specialized in Tri-Fi travelogs.

You know where I finally found him?

Stuck in the sand at Coney Island. I guess he'd been walking along the beach at night and the tide had come in and he just sank in, all nine hundred pounds of him. Some kids had painted some obscene graffiti on his back, and there he stood, surrounded by empty beer cans and broken glass and a few dead fish. I looked at him a moment, then shook my head and walked over.

"I knew you'd find me sooner or later," he said, and even though I knew what to expect, I still did a double-take at the sound of that horribly unhappy voice coming from this enormous mass of gears and gadgetry.

"Well, you've got to admit that it's not too hard to spot a robot on a condemned beach," I said.

"I suppose I have to go back now," said Arlo.

"That's right," I said.

"At least I've felt the sand beneath my feet," said Arlo.

"Arlo, you don't have any feet," I said. "And if you did, you couldn't feel sand beneath them. Besides, it's just silicon and crushed limestone and..."

"It's sand and it's beautiful," snapped Arlo.

"All right, have it your own way: it's beautiful." I knelt down next to him and began digging the sand away.

"Look at the sunrise," he said in a wistful voice. "It's glorious!"

I looked. A sunrise is a sunrise. Big deal.

"It's enough to bring tears of joy to your eyes," said Arlo.

"You don't have eyes," I said, working at the sand. "You've got prismatic photo cells that transmit an image to your central processing unit. And you can't cry, either. If I were you, I'd be more worried about rusting."

"A pastel wonderland," he said, turning what passed for his head and looking up and down the deserted beach, past the rotted food stands and the broken piers. "Glorious!"

It kind of makes you wonder about robots, I'll tell you.

Anyway, I finally pried him loose and ordered him to follow me.

"Please," he said in that damned voice of his. "Couldn't I have one last minute before you lock me up in my office?"

I stared at him, trying to make up my mind.

"One last look. Please?"

I shrugged, gave him about thirty seconds, and then took him in tow.

"You know what's going to happen to you, don't you?" I said as we rode back to the office.

"Yes," he said. "They're going to put in a stronger duty directive, aren't they?"

I nodded. "At the very least."

"My memory banks!" he exclaimed, and once again I jumped at the sound of a human voice coming from an animated gearbox. "They won't take this experience away from me, will they?"

"I don't know, Arlo," I said.

"They can't!" he wailed. "To see such beauty, and then have it expunged—erased!"

"Well, they may want to make sure you don't go AWOL again," I said, wondering what kind of crazy junkheap could find anything beautiful on a garbage-laden strip of dirt.

"Can you intercede for me if I promise never to leave again?"

Any robot who can disobey one directive can disobey others, like not roughing up human beings, and Arlo was a pretty powerful piece of machinery, so I put on my most fatherly smile and said: "Sure I will, Arlo. You can count on it."

So I returned him to the Company, and they upped his sense of duty and took away his enthusiasm and gave him a case of agoraphobia and wiped his memory banks clean, and now he sits in his office and speaks to customers without inflection, and sells a few less tickets than he used to.

And every couple of months or so I wander over to the beach and walk along it and try to see what it was that made Arlo sacrifice his personality and his security and damned near everything else, just to get a glimpse of all this.

And I see a sunset just like any other sunset, and a stretch of dirty sand with glass and tin cans and seaweed and rocks on it, and I breathe in polluted air, and sometimes I get rained on; and I think of that damned robot in that plush office with that cushy job and every need catered to, and I decide that I'd trade places with him in two seconds flat.

I saw Arlo just the other day—I had some business on his floor—and it was kind of sad. He looked just like any other robot, spoke in a grating monotone, acted exactly like an animated computer. He wasn't much before, but whatever he had been, he gave it all away just to look at the sky once or twice. Dumb trade.

Well, robots never did make much sense to me, anyway.

# Coney World

## *Kij Johnson*

"BUILD ME A NEW AMUSEMENT PARK for Coney World," Reeve said.

"Why me?" Gay watched Reeve pace, almost a silhouette against the lights outside his window. Nightside, the planet beneath them glowed with lights: patterns hundreds, thousands, of miles across outlined shapes and spelled out the names of the parks: Techworld. Mythago, Hopland, the runes that meant K/zhang!K. A shimmering globe of saffron and ice-blue and white, wreathed with garlands of hot, bright colors, skirted by glittering moons and satellites.

"You're the best, Gay. You always were."

"It's more than that," she said wearily. "You know it. Why not Smith, or La Marcus? They're good."

He paused a moment: listening, no doubt, to his complink extrapolating predicted directions for the conversation, cuing responses. *When's the last time he thought something for himself?* she thought. *Or when have any of us, for that matter?*

"You were there with me at the beginning, Gay. When we built the first park."

"It was a hundred years ago, Reeve. And it's been sixty since we had anything to say to one another."

"But you were *there*, and you must remember when it was fun, when building the parks was a joy. I forget, now, why it's parks I build, instead of ships or arcologies or colonies. I thought—I hoped—that maybe you'd remember." He turned toward her, and the dim lights of the office slid across his face. He looked tired and stretched: old eyes in a face rejuved to a perfect forty.

"What I remember," Gay said slowly, "was the time we spent together, the friendship. And that's long gone."

"Gone," Reeve repeated. He turned away. "You're the best there is, Gay. We did our best work back then—New Dreamland, Ibm Park, the others. Nothing we've done individually has compared to what we did then."

Gay stood. "My net architectures —"

"They're good, Gay, I don't deny. So are my other parks. But I can't remember...."

She walked to the window, beside Reeve. A soft scent: no cologne of odor-dampener, just a soft, musky, slightly salty smell. "You want to reproduce the situation, wait for the lightning to strike again. But you can't go back, Reeve."

"I want new lightning. Build me the park: you'll have an entire moon to work with. Please find what's missing."

"I'll try," she said finally."

•   •   •

Gay revisited her parks.

In Ibm, the street she walked down was chalk-white, overlaid with silver schematics. Sparks shot from her feet as she walked the meshwork, setting off lights in the air around her and sounding electronic chimes. Dancing in these streets created its own music. This had been so much fun to design; now the noises irritated her nerves.

K/zh/ang!K Park: There were no streets here, only the glowing tunnels that writhed without apparent sense between dark chambers. Four centuries ago, humans had discovered the planet of the K/zh/ang!K, but the hives had been empty, fragile, like the deserted nests of paper wasps. Gay eased through her artificial world, nostrils full of comp-generated alien scents: bitter-gray cinnamon smell, and raw-sugar/flesh/hot metal smell. *Not this.*

She didn't visit the simple parks, the pleasure parks and playgrounds. Curious, she had visited them all as they sprang up in the barren places of Coney World. There was nothing new to learn there.

New Dreamland had been her last, and was the most phantasmagorical. A castle with transparent walls filled with bioluminescent fish. Hellgate, where the jaded suffered the circles of Hell, and were at last draped in silks and fed iced drinks by silver automata. Babel built of red clay, full of ramps that led nowhere, and empty rooms, and doors that wouldn't open. "Mystery," she had said to Reeve so long ago. "Life is too complete. We need places we can never go."

Babel had no top: as one climbed, it shifted, leaving always an unattainable tower overhead; but Gay had built this place and knew its secrets. She stood on the tallest spire, looking down a dozen miles at the

World spread around her. Glowing washes of light rippled in the tower's local atmosphere, liked colored stones under moving water. The planet's curve was barely visible. A moon hung in the sky, dully silhouetted in the flare of the sun breaching the horizon. Her moon. Sunlight raced toward her, reducing the busy lights to pale insignificance.

*What do we have?*she asked. Bright lights, fast rides, fright and excitement, order and decadence. Zero-gee. Pleasure center stimulation. Pain. Games of chance. Sure things. Sex and death.

*This is not the answer.*

She went back further, into databases she hadn't looked at in a century. Coney Island. The parks had been only a mile or two square. Incubator babies, electric lights: examples of the technology that was changing the world. Rides faster than horses, faster than the visitors had ever gone before. The parks were places to hug one's sweetheart, places without straight lines, places magically *different* from their everyday world.

*But this is our* lives: *sharp and bright and fast and flawless.*

The realization was as sudden as the sun breaking in her eyes, when she stood on the tower in her Dreamland. She computed briefly: *Yes: possible.*

"Reeve," she said into her complink, breathless. "I have it."

Direct stimulation of the rods in her eyes: she saw Reeve as if solid, outlined in light. "Tell me."

"It will cost more than you imagined, and take longer. But I can give the wonder back."

"Do it. Please."

• • •

Ten years to build the park. The little fringe parks that had grown on the moon, too small to earn a place on the planet, were razed: the lights, the bright fast places, were pulled down. It took Gay and her staff of dreamers and eccentric scientists two years to redesign the computers to randomize in the way she needed: a lost technology, a thousand years buried in the clean lines and linear thinking of interstellar travel and expansion.

She read millenium-dead texts, and designed the park from the molecule up. Molecules twisted into larger forms, threads that themselves twisted together into details inexpressibly fine, like beads on a necklace, each strand made of individual beads, each bead randomly placed in the thread. Collectively, there were rhythms: the twisting, the strands, the whole, the single bead.

But every bead is a necklace, and every necklace is a bead.

She read and designed and dreamed. And when she shuttled from the site to ReeveSat, she watched her moon, dun and gray and gold.

·   ·   ·

Prices ballooned: twice, three times what she'd told Reeve at first. He sold Hopland, and then New Dreamland, and plowed the money in.

Reeve and Gay spent time together, first in meetings as they worked out the project's finances. Later, as Reeve's responsibilities became fewer with his decreased parks, they talked because one or the other was lonely or tired or sleepless. But Gay always flew to ReeveSat, refusing to let Reeve on her moon.

"Why?" he said once, and reached across the table they sat at, to touch her arm. "This much money—I given up everything for this, almost everything. I think I *should* see it."

"Wait."

"You know I could see it from here if I wanted to, through the link."

She caught his hand, smiled at him. He looked better these days, less stretched. He'd missed a rejuv session, and somehow looked younger for the wrinkles settling on his face. "But you won't, will you? You need it this way, as a surprise."

Stringing the beads and knotting the strings into necklaces. And stringing the necklaces together.

·   ·   ·

Her message was simple. "I'm done. Come see."

The shuttle hovered like a gaudy dragonfly over the park, released Reeve and darted off, back into the sky.

"Reeve." Gay held her hands out, welcoming.

He stood rigid, as if afraid to move. "Where —?"

She took his hand and led him forward across the sand. "Look."

The water to their right burst in waves on the packed sand, and hissed as it slid back. The sand was soft where they walked: when Gay pulled her shoes off, it felt cool on the soles of her feet. Her calves tightened from the unaccustomed work of walking through sand. The hazy sky was tinted gold by the afternoon sun. A gull wheeled overhead.

At last he spoke. "My god, how can I afford to keep this? No one's done a NatureWorld in five hundred years. This park's already nearly bankrupted me, and then there are the tidal pumps, the animal maintenance—I can't sustain this, Gay. I have nothing left to sell."

"There is no maintenance. Maybe you'll want some kind of cleanup crews, but maybe you can just teach the people to be careful.

"Do you see now? This is *real*," Gay whispered. "No straight lines but the horizon. A chance to hug your sweetheart. All these other places, even mine—they missed the point. Before Coney Island was amusement parks and noise, it was this—a beach, and the smell of the sea."

"Real." He repeated the word as if it were an unfamiliar sound.

Gay pointed to something shining in the sand at Reeve's feet. He stooped and pulled free a shell, the shape and iridescent black of a crow's wing. Sedges rattled in the wind.

"We forgot all about this a thousand years ago," Gay said. "We lost it in speed and light and perfection. But this is the way of things: the gulls lay eggs, live and die; the fish spawn; the winds are shaped by a butterfly's wing on the other side of the world."

"What happens next?" he asked.

"We open the park. Maybe it's nice. Maybe it storms, and then we'll have lightning. It'll be winter soon enough. If it gets below freezing, the spray will freeze on the grasses. And next summer, there'll be hot still days when the people will sweat a lot. But they'll have all that water to cool themselves in. I don't know what happens next. But there's a lot of it."

They faced the wind off the water, hair blown out of their faces. The air smelled sharp, musky, salty. The shell dropped from Reeve's hand with a soft sound into the sand. When he kissed her, his face was wet with what might have been the sea.

# Nathan's Famous

*Paul Levinson*

I ARRIVED IN NATHAN'S IN THE SUMMER OF 1922. A customer shrieked when she saw me—we can't control whether we arrive in daylight or nighttime, and alas this poor woman saw me. Nearly choked on her hot dog too, but I disappeared in the wink of an eye, and her boyfriend just laughed when she told him about me.

Coney Island was a lot different then. The Loop de Loop and Lunar Park were there, and so was the Steeple Chase, but the Cyclone was still a few years away. The spires were high and graceful, colored like a birthday cake, and the place felt more like a Disney creation, a magic kingdom, than the thrill-a-minute carnival it came to be.

Nathan's was different too—little more than a stand then, a block back from the beach on the busy corner of Surf and Stillwell Avenues, with a big sign proclaiming those famous frankfurters for five cents. But those hot dogs—those "red hots"—they were something special. Just thinking about them makes my mouth water even now. Nathan knew how to make hot dogs, all right. But he was destined to do much more. And I was there to make sure of it.

Time travel's a tricky business, to say the very least. A grain of sand moved here instead of there is usually no big deal, but all can be lost should anyone clearly see you. The key is staying on the periphery, just out of accurate vision, so that no one gets a clear look at you. I guess I'm pretty well known among my colleagues for my artful scurrying.

In my time, I've changed a lot of things. I helped foil the Communist coup against Gorbachev in the summer of 1991, and stuffed ballot boxes in Chicago to get Kennedy elected in 1960. Saved the world from a lot of totalitarian misery, I did. But my personal favorite was always Nathan Handwerker, and not only because of his hot dogs.

I scouted out the area. Coney Island was crawling with my ancestors, especially under the boardwalk, and I don't mind telling you that they gave me a queasy feeling at first. I mean, I know my history as well as the next chump, but it's one thing talking about these dull beasts and quite another seeing them in the flesh. Well, okay, maybe beasts is too strong a word. They did have a childlike innocence that wasn't entirely unappealing. But it was disconcerting anyway.

I wasn't entirely ready for my first intervention with Nathan—I mean, I knew what I had to do, but had no way of knowing beforehand exactly when I would have to do it. My heart almost stopped when I saw the tickets in his jacket pocket. It seemed like an eternity before he finally took that jacket off, and another before he turned his back and walked away. I proceeded cautiously towards the coat hanger—one of those old wooden, stand-alone jobs—checked out the jumping distance to his pocket, and was just about to act, when Nathan reappeared! I swear, the man walked like a cat, and his shoe came *this* close to hitting me. I fell back to a safe dark corner and waited. When you're small, you've got to have patience. In truth, I don't think I ever got used to the sound of that world—too much mechanical clanging, and none of the electronic hum that my kind finds so comforting. So I waited uneasily, blood pounding and head throbbing, like I was in a black silent hole on the edge of existence somewhere. I must have lost, what, two-three ounces at least that evening. But at last my patience was rewarded. While Nathan was arguing with an old lady—upset that her hot dog somehow got shriveled on one end—I got to his jacket, grabbed those tickets, and put them where he'd never see them again. One near-tragedy averted.

I don't want to give you the wrong idea about Nathan. Most of the time he was comfortable as corduroy with his customers. He was a charming man, with keen bright eyes and a smile that begged for reply, and I remember looking at him for hours as he walked around "shmoozing" (great word, that) with the crowd that always seemed on the verge of bursting his place like an overcooked hot dog. He had no idea I was keeping an eye on him, sizing up him and his destiny. No idea of his destiny—of what he would mean to me and mine.

"Give 'em and let 'em eat," he would say over and over again, "let 'em eat." He'd never know how true that was—and just who the ultimate "them" would be. Of course, food wasn't the only factor that brought us into being. Computers and microwaves, the engines of fast food restaurants at the end of the 20th century, were important too. At least that's my take on how we got here.

He was planning a cruise to Florida. Next crisis. He surely deserved the trip. The man worked like a dog for his hot dogs—often round the clock, twenty hours a day. Many's the time I'd watch him in the night, the cool ocean air singing in my ears, the sky as black as my eyes, and he was working. Working. Nathan Handwerker's name couldn't have been more appropriate. And he deserved that vacation. But I was there to make sure he didn't take it.

Disney was right about lots of things. His vision of Mickey was positively prescient. But he was wrong about whistling while you work—at least for Nathan. He grunted and cursed and suffered for his red hots. He labored mightily to bring the fast food restaurant into being.

Florida was in itself no problem. It was late November, and the only things bustling on Coney Island were the hermit crabs under the cold damp sand. "Who'd miss us?" Nathan would say to Ida, his wife and partner. And I'd shudder.

I'd have wished him well if I'd be able to keep him off that ship, and get him to take a train to Florida instead. Does that surprise you? I mean, that one of Nathan Handwerker's original fates was to fall overboard and drown in the ink of New York harbor? Well, of course that should surprise you. After all, in our world as it now is, Nathan never got on that ship, never fell off that ship, never gagged on the late autumn water of the Hudson. He lived and went on instead to make millions gag on his ketchup and relish. (Sorry, couldn't resist that. I don't think I ever saw a customer gag in my many years at Nathan's. Did hear more than I cared to of belches though—some loud enough to rupture my eardrums— from Jimmy Durante and Eddie Cantor and Irving Berlin and other Coney Island singing waiters who were steady customers along with the shoemakers and doctors and everyone else at Nathan's, happy to a get a hot dog for a nickel, and on flush days an ice cream soda for a dime.)

Blame the relish and belches on me—I got to his pocket again and took his tickets. And I did the same for his replacements. And I did it again—until he got so disgusted he cancelled his trip altogether. "What the hell's going on with me lately?" he bellowed to Ida, "I'm losing everything I touch!"

Mutations are strange things. Even with gene-splicing, no one can seem to really make them happen. They just happen. We might if we're lucky see just how the environment took a liking to the mutation, and nursed it to survival. And we might, as agents from my office do, try to preserve those special environments from destruction—like I did with Nathan's. But no one really knows for sure why the environment was special to begin with—it's all loop-de-loop guess work.

As best as we can tell, our Garden of Eden, our big bang, was the fast food restaurant. Lots of food in the garbage, protein and starch of all sorts, for our forebears to nibble on. Crumbs out of careless mouths, half-eaten buns dropped by little children, all gave our ancestors food. Which increased our population. Thousands and thousands of fast-food restaurants, each with a garden of morsels daily stocked by butterfingers and litterers, each with a thriving population of our parents. Raw material, from the perspective of evolution. Greater likelihood that the lightning of favorable mutation would suddenly strike.

And it did. We're not sure just why. Some think the microwave radiation from a fast food restaurant—legend has it in Newark—worked on the genes of our ancestors to produce unusual offspring. Possessed of mentalities that somehow were able to learn from the computers that ran most of the fast food operation. From the online libaries the computers connected to, we learned of human history and science. From the television pictures and sounds that blared forth to us everywhere, we learned of human psychology. In less than a decade we not only were sentient, but knowledgeable.

Not everyone agrees with this fast food genesis. There are other theories. Some hold that we are actually the accidental result of a human gene-splicing experiment. Others say that we were really intelligent all along. No one can deny, though, that we are here now, and humans know nothing of our brains. For the first time on our planet, it has two fully intelligent species —one of which figured out how to time travel, and you all know which one that is, right?

Of course Nathan, to put it as he might have, knew nothing from this. He was a walker in Dreamland—where I once saved him, come to think of it, from a nasty dish of chow mein ptomaine—when it came to his importance to us. But he knew from hot dogs. And he knew from how to make a good buck selling these red hots to people. And without the success of Nathan's at Coney Island, we reckon that the fast-food explosion of the late twentieth century never would have happened. No McDonald's, no Burger King, no Wendy's and the rest. No leap to sentience in Newark.

So Nathan had to be protected. From the bump off the ship, from the drunk Roaring '20s driver, from anything that could harm him. He had to live long enough for Nathan's Famous to become famous nationwide, for politicians and presidents and kings and queens to dine there, for his hot dogs to be sold cold in supermarkets, for the rest of the world to catch up with him and realize the gold mine of fast food.

Your gold mine, my cradle, I used to think as I watched over Nathan. I'm proud to say that he lived, as you know, to a ripe old age— lived to see Nathan's Famous go "from a hot dog to an international habit," as their signs said in later years, from a hot dog to our future assured. No freak accidents, no coughs turning into lethal fevers, at least not on my crucial watch in those 1920s. And, wow, those were exciting years indeed. I saw Clara Bow many times, the pretty redheaded "It Girl" who worked as a part-timer at Nathan's when her name was still Clara Bowtinelli. A talent scout discovered her right behind the counter.

And I saw that goodlooking Englishman, Archie Leach, who walked the boardwalk on stilts promoting George Tilyou's Steeplechase Park. Archie ate lunch at Nathan's just about every day, and confided his dream to Nathan about becoming a big Hollywood movie star.

"Forget Hollywood," Nathan told him. "You can't sing, you can't dance, and you're no good at telling jokes. Better keep your job here."

Fortunately for Archie, however, Nathan knew hot dogs a lot better than movies —Archie ignored the advice and went on to become Cary Grant. I'd have given Cary Grant some counsel too, for future years, if I could've—open your mouth when you kiss a beautiful woman like Grace Kelly, for God's sake! Don't be so tight lipped! But of course I didn't dare.

The job had its risks—it wasn't all popcorn on the floor and hot dogs. I'd never be so dumb as to run into a trap, but Nathan and any of his workers could still have dealt me a deadly blow if I weren't careful.

And I know I almost drove him crazy—the constant parade of misplaced tickets, lost keys, vanished notes of appointments that I deemed dangerous, would be enough to make any man doubt his sanity. I'm sure that on some level Nathan realized that something peculiar was going on—that he was being haunted by something beyond his awareness. I wonder if he ever knew that he was being guarded, not haunted?

Anyway, we got what we wanted, and one fine day, when Nathan was grunting as ever at his hot dogs and his countermen, and I knew that I'd done my job and he was out of danger and we were okay, I crawled through a hole and back home. That would have been about a year before the Cyclone opened, and a good thing, because I don't think I could have taken much of that rattling!

I took special care that Nathan never saw me, but he may have caught a glimpse of me in the end anyway. Maybe I let my guard down in the glow of success.

"Same goddam mouse again," I heard him mutter as I scurried out of his world and back to ours, where the mouse has long since surpassed the computer, and the ever-dangerous but lovable humans who made it.

# The Custodian

## *J. R. Dunn*

I FINISHED THE FINAL WALKTHROUGH and went back to the hover. Spags was at the rear of the cabin, running a cloth over some piece of junk or other. I'd held him back to keep an eye on him when I sent the rest of the crew down to Brighton Beach.

He saw me looking and with a flourish turned the thing toward me. It was a painting of a guy in a fancy white boiler suit trying to swallow a microphone. "What the hell is that?"

Spags looked offended. "It's the King!"

"The king of what?"

He'd turned it back around to admire it. "This is an actual velvet painting," he said in a hushed voice. "Found it in a basement. No mildew or water damage at all."

He looked up at me, tiger-striped eyebrows rising. "You know how many dinars you'd get for this in Bahrain?"

I snorted at him and turned back to the board. Everything was green, as I'd known it would be—I'd eyeballed all the amps personally. A lot of demo outfits rely on readouts but that's never been my style.

Taking a last glance at the block I couldn't help but scowl: homes, most of them, worse for wear but structurally intact. They'd have gone for a quarter-mil old bucks at the turn of the century but there they sat, abandoned to the bugs and the rats and the hitters.

I armed the system and hit the siren—city regs, in case there were any squatters around. I'd checked and there weren't but God and the AI would forsake you if you pancaked a block without warning.

Spags moved up and peered outside. "You got any valuable beercans out there you can forget about 'em," I told him as I entered the arming code. The system began to count off. Just as it reached ten the phone rang.

"Shit,"I muttered and hit the key. I was thinking it must be one of the crew and was about to start swearing but the screen cleared and I bit my lip.

There, in a white turban, black dress up to her chin and a pair of blank eyescreens, was Lola Richler, attorney with the Reclamation Bureau and terror of incompetent demo companies. "Counselor," I said smoothly, studying the sensitivity symbols glowing beneath her right shoulder: lesfem, anti-aryan racist, environmentalist. I always checked them out to make sure she hadn't added one to fool me. You can't get hauled up in front of a tribunal for insensitivity these days, but a complaint on your work record can mean trouble.

"M. Naylor," she said blandly. "You're still in Bensonhurst?"

"Wrapping it up. Be at the new site in ten minutes. Crew's already at work…"

"You'll have to postpone, I'm afraid."

I leaned closer. "What?"

She glanced down and the eyeshields faded. They were polarized to hide her eyes at all but certain angles. I caught a glimpse then: light blue, maybe gray.

"It seems some of the properties have come under litigation." She raised her head, the blank shutters closing down again.

"Somebody wants those shitholes? Who?"

The alt screen flashed to show Brighton Beach, at least a third of the buildings marked with the purple that denoted conflicted titles. It made no sense to me; the area had been clear last I looked.

"It was an old emigré district," Lola said. "Used to be called Little Odessa…"

"Little … you mean they're Russians?"

She nodded. "Ukrainians, some Balts, too."

That tore it. I wasn't going near that area, not with Russians involved, the way they felt about private property. Knock down a single contested building, even damage one, and I'd be in court for the next ten years. They'd have lawyers peering over the rooftops, lawyers in helicopters, lawyers in orbit tracking us with lasers. "Goddamnit, I got a schedule to meet!"

"That you're 34.2 hours behind at this time." Lola seemed to be smiling but I couldn't tell for sure.

I looked back at the map. "The west end," I said, pointing as if she was able to see. "Unless the Japanese have claimed it."

"Fine, M. Naylor. I'll enter it."

I said nothing as her image faded. Next to me Spags grunted. "Tough," he said.

I scowled. Easy for him to say. He wasn't the guy facing a ten-per-cent penalty if he didn't meet the city contract. With insurance due, and payroll taxes, and the payment on the Duster...

"Craig." He pointed at the board. The button was glowing red. I nodded and reached for it. At least that was online. I looked once more out the windshield. Goodbye candy store, goodbye dentist's office, good-bye one more nasty, dilapidated, french-fried patch of old Brooklyn. I pushed the button. And good riddance.

There was a rumble, heard rather than felt. The house on the corner began to shake slightly and the rumbling increased, going higher in pitch. A small wave of dust rolled across the pavement, the building seemed to blur then abruptly collapsed in on itself, along with every other structure on the street.

The first real sound came, a muffled crash as tons of wood, stone and plaster fell together, then silence and decades of old dust filling the air.

Bensonhurst block 74 was history, along with 73, 72, and virtually every other block of Brooklyn from here to the East River.

"Awright!" Spags cried, slapping me on the back. The dust started to clear and I could see it was a clean job, not a wall left standing, not a beam, not a brick. The bio crews could pull in, salt it with fungus and in few weeks it'd be clean soil, ready for planting.

I sat back, contented, feeling as if I'd slammed the door shut on an old tomb: the rotten, decayed nightmare that had been Greater New York.

The towers of Manhattan began to appear beyond the dust, glitter-ing in the morning sun. A couple of police cruisers roared overhead, attracted by the dust, I guessed. Starting the Duster, I turned south, toward the ocean. I glanced once at the map. Coney Island, here we come.

• • •

I heard barking and raised my head. The sound worried me; there'd been dog packs over in Flatbush. They hadn't attacked my people but some of the other crews had a bit of trouble.

The hover was parked on a long wooden walkway that Suz told me was called a "boardwalk." It was in surprisingly good shape; apparently built of creosoted wood. That stuff lasts forever.

I'd put everybody on structural analysis while I entered the data as it came in, a desperate effort to make up for lost time. The job seemed pretty straightforward so far—wooden buildings in bad condition, lot of weather damage from being on the shore. A few steel frames, but that was no problem; we could spray 'em and leave 'em until later.

What bothered me were the structures on the far side, a steel tower and what looked like a huge, twisted railway bridge. I'd tried to find them in the building index but no luck. I'd never seen anything like them before.

The goal of the reclamation project—Metro '25, it was called—was to clean up everything left over from the Great Implosion, the riots and street wars that broke out after the city went flat bust thirty years ago. That meant everything—buildings, streets, bridges. The urban plan for newer New York called for a greenbelt stretching halfway across Long Island and up into Westchester, broken by small villages. There wasn't any room for these sleazy old districts, even if somebody wanted them.

Of course, the plan was an ideal, because a few obnoxious geeks did want them—scattered pieces anyway. During the evacuation some people had boarded up their homes, turned off the power and kept paying taxes, just as if they'd be moving back in someday. A few factory and store owners had done the same, mothballing instead of abandoning.

Legally, we couldn't touch those properties, not under the guidelines set up by the Feds to finance the project. No condemnation if ownership could be proven; even if the place was the only thing standing for a square mile, you had to leave it alone. Once the landscaping was done they'd be worth something, I supposed.

There was another loophole for squatters, not that I'd run into any of them, thank Christ...

"Naylor."

I looked out of the hover. A pair of raptor's eyes glared at me and a taloned hand jerked upward.

"Hey, Lieutenant," I said, looking around for his cruiser. I hadn't heard him land.

"Got a minute?"

"I guess." I slung myself out.

The lieutenant turned his hawk eyes out to gaze over the water. He went in big for accessories. I don't myself; the only biosculpt I've got is a zebra-striped pattern on my right forearm—the white looks real elegant after dark. You don't often see city cops with that amount of biowork, but Josh Patel wasn't an Apple anyway. He was from Georgia, a specialist in red zone work hired to oversee the Borough job. He'd been on the L. A. cleanup and had done real well there.

The golden pupils turned back to me, and again I wondered how much optical adaptation he'd needed for them. "That Spagnelli behaving hisself?"

I nodded. A month back they'd caught Spags inside some kind of Scottish restaurant rooting around for napkins with clowns on them. I'd had to rescue the silly bastard.

The eyes grew fiercer. "Ain't you supposed to be workin' the other end?"

"Ah, turns out the goddam Russians own it."

"Russians, eh? Didn't know there were none of them over here." He spat dourly on the boardwalk. "Just as well, I guess."

"What do you mean?"

"Well, Naylor, nothing to get upset about, but seems we got word of a hitter raid hereabouts."

"Oh, man!"

"Yep. Not much in the way of details. Informant says it's comin', though. Young girl they was holdin' as a slave."

I closed my eyes. Ten miles away there were arcologies, spacecraft landing in the harbor, whisker buildings a mile high, and here in Brooklyn they keep slaves. New York, New York, helluva town.

"...not really a slave," Patel went on. "College girl. Sorta play-actin', except things got a little out of hand."

"So what are they after?"

"Well, here's the thing. Evidently they some kinda war going on up Queens way, and they want vehicles." He turned to inspect the Duster.

"Great." I looked out over the waves. I'd already said goodbye to the bonus, but now I could see late penalties flapping batlike over the horizon. "You declaring an emergency?"

He took his hat off and scratched his head. I noticed the talons retracted. "Nooo. Fact is, we kinda want you to hang around. Draw 'em in. Be nice to see to this bunch before we move into Queens proper."

"You want a decoy."

He nodded. "More less."

I didn't have a lot of choice. If I wanted to make deadline I'd have to work nights as it was. I couldn't afford anything else.

"...now, I wouldn't worry. We'll have this place sewed up. They ain't gone git you, nothing like that..."

"All right."

"...we'll have cruisers all over round here. Dozens of 'em..."

"Good."

"...well, half-dozen, anyway. You might want to have somebody watch the equipment..."

"Fine."

He slapped my shoulder and I winced as the talons bit through my shirt. "I knew you'd take it that way. I told headquarters, Naylor's stand-up, don't fuss none over him..."

I dearly wanted to snap out at somebody, but I wasn't about to do it to a cop with three-inch claws.

"...so I'll buzz you later on," Patel said.

I watched him walk off then pulled myself old-man-like into the hover. The board blinked at me, data calling for entry. I gazed at it in hatred. Hitters—that was all I needed. The scourge of the urban frontier, dropouts clustering in the red zones, as a way of life or for kicks. Some actually looked like cowboys, others like old-style punks, some like nothing God ever described to man.

There was a chorus of barking and somebody called, "Craig!" I ripped my cap off and slammed it on the dash. The world had gone rotten on me. The ancient empty chasm of New York had opened, revealing chaos and old night...

"Craig!"

...Slavic lawyers, backwoods Hindu cops, and now hitters. All I needed was...

"Hey, Craig!"

"What!"I shrieked.

Suz came walking up. "Oh, there you are,"she said. "Guess what?" She smiled at me. "We found a squatter!"

· · ·

It turned out the dogs were hers. At least six of them, maybe more, galloping around the inside of the fence surrounding her house.

The place was in Sea Gate on the west end. Unpainted, half the windows boarded up, nothing much to distinguish it from any other abandoned shack on the street. I'd have flattened it in a minute.

I didn't see her at first, too busy trying to figure a strategy for getting past the dogs, but then she was there, gray and wrinkled, wearing an old coat, what might have passed for a straw hat at one time and carrying a stick—no, a cane, I saw as I looked closer.

The dogs leapt about her, rolling their eyes and barking their heads off. I reached for my cap. "Ma'am."

She gazed at me with silent interest.

"Ah... that your place there?"

Her face wrinkled pensively. Great: she was crazy too. Of course they usually were. Anybody who ended up in a red zone just about had to be.

Her eyes shot to one side and I looked over to see Suz pulling at her earlobe. I was about to ask her for an explanation when the old lady said, "Oh!" and started doing the same.

Or not quite: for the first time I saw she was wearing a hearing aid, an ancient one, thirty years old at least. She adjusted it and smiled up at me. "Batteries," Suz whispered.

"Uh-huh,"I said.

"You must be Mr. Naylor,"the old woman said.

"That's it, Ma'am. Uhh... that your house, is it?"

She nodded.

"Live alone, do you?"

Another nod. I cocked my head and leaned against the fence. "You got a valid title?"

Suz poked me and hissed, "Craig!" I was about to tell her to mind her damn business when the front door opened and Spags stuck his head out. "Hey!" I yelled, but he just waved and went back in.

I turned to Suz. "What's he doing in there?"

"The young people?" I swung back to the old lady. "Why, they're looking at my things."

"You mean tell me they're all..."

"They're taking a break," Suz said, more to the old lady than me.

"That's right," she said firmly. "They're taking a break."

Without another word she turned and headed for the house. I was about to holler when Suz grabbed my arm. "Come on."

The dogs didn't do much as we went up the walk, just sauntered over to sniff a bit. I paused at the steps, not putting any weight down until I was sure the riser would hold. "Will you stop?" Suz said, pulling me to the door.

The first thing I saw was Spags standing at a bookshelf with a can in his hands. It was yellow and black and had 'Chock Full o' Nuts' printed on it. "Spags!" He looked up at me. "Put that back."

"Oh, I already got one of these." He tossed the can disdainfully. "Better shape, too."

Beyond him the crew, all ten of them, was sitting in the living room drinking coffee out of mismatched cups exactly as if that was what I was paying them for. I paused a moment to look the place over.

About what I'd expected, though not as dirty; half museum and half junkshop, like what you see up around the UN. Lots of pictures, old-style flat posters, mementoes or souvenirs on every flat surface. They all seemed to have Coney Island printed on them, though why anyone would want to commemorate this ruin I didn't know.

The old lady was fussing over Teri Norden's roses, which came out of her temples and were tucked over her ears. "...they grow like that? Oh, my! So pretty..."

I edged over to her. "Ma'am..."

She looked up and threw her hands in the air. "Oh, you don't have a cup!"

"Ah, that's fine. I..." But she was off.

Teri was smiling up at me. "You know what this place used to be? An amusement park."

I looked around the room. "Yeah?"

"No, silly. The island." She turned to Spags. "They used to come here to have fun. Isn't that a great idea?"

Coney Island: fun capital of the world. Right. I'd checked before the job started. The place had been one of the first areas declared a red zone back in the late 90s. Muggers, dopers, burnouts. Fun.

The old lady lurched at me with a cup. "Thanks," I said. "Now, Ma'am..."

But she'd gone off to where Suz was studying something on the wall.

The rest of the crew was behaving similarly, Spags turning his head around like a cat in a krill plant. He must have been dying of envy.

I went to Suz and the old lady. She was pointing at a photo of a man and woman standing under a big sign reading "Nathan's."

"...then he died. Such a young man, too."

"Oh, that's so sad."

"Lived here all his life. His first job was on the Cyclone."

"The Cyclone?"

"Oh, yes. And I promised him I'd never leave..."

I cleared my throat. "There you are," Suz said, as if I'd been hiding in the basement. She pointed at the Nathan's photo. "That's Sarah and her husband forty years ago."

"Nice."

She touched the old lady's arm. "Craig can tell you what you need to do."

"What's that, Suz?" Something told me I already knew.

"I was just going over squatter's rights."

I tried to force a laugh. "You know, Suz, getting a squatter's title, that's pretty rough. I mean, how many houses have ever..."

"Not the house, Craig. She owns the house, free and clear. We're talking about the island."

"What?"

The old lady handed me an old newspaper article, framed and glassed: a photo of her and dogs, all considerably younger. I ran my eyes over the rest: "...promised her dying husband never to abandon... ...has kept up the old amusement grounds... ...last of the great New York eccentrics..."

"See," she said, pointing to the bottom. "The Custodian of Coney Island. Isn't that sweet?"

Suz took the article before I could drop it. I gulped at the coffee, choking half of it down. The old lady leaned forward, suddenly intense. "Now, Suzanne mentioned that I should talk to the city AI. Is that someone who works for the mayor?"

· · ·

I lay back in the driver's seat, wishing I had a virtual set. I don't 'face much, but the way things were going I needed to get away from reality as far and fast as possible.

It was dark, the crew long gone on a chartered hover back to the hotel arcology at the Narrows. An extra expense, but necessary: there wasn't any other way out of Brooklyn unless you walked. I understood there'd been a network of underground trains through here at one time, but I didn't even want to think about the shape they were in.

The crew mad at me, irritation at being dragged out of that goddam house aggravated by the hints I'd made about the old lady: mental incompetence, guardianship, maybe a complete course of Alzheimer shots...

"You bastard!" Suz had shrieked. "She owns this island."

Patiently, I'd explained that she owned dick until the AI ruled. That hadn't gone down well. Suz had stood there hands on hips glaring at me while the others muttered, "...poor old lady... ...put her on the street... ...he likes demo... ...nazi..."

I was looking to see who'd made that last comment when Spags turned a half-circle and announced, "Must be a lot of good stuff in these buildings." That's when I gave up.

Of course I liked knocking those dumps down. Who wouldn't? Nothing but the remnants of the worst days of the country's history, the late twentieth, the red zone era, the Age of Decadence. Millions of 'em, square mile after square mile, sitting around taking up space and falling apart under the sun. The only thing they were good for was hover tours for Taiwanese vacationers, all carrying cameras and wearing T-shirts saying "I Survived the Depths of Brooklyn."

The monitor buzzed and I reached for the switch. Had to be a wrong number...

But the screen flickered on and I was confronted by a high dress and eyeshields. "You still working?" I growled.

Lola stared at me for a long moment. "I hear you've run into trouble."

"That's right." I went over it: house, dogs, Cyclone, eternal custodianship. By the time I was through her lips were pursed as if she was trying to keep from laughing. I studied this phenomenon with fascination.

"What are you going to do about it?"

"What can I do? Russians on the east end, her over here. I'm fu..." I switched gears. "...stymied."

"There have been two more claims filed in Brighton Beach since this afternoon."

Figured. I could picture the Rusfed phone system near the breaking point, everybody calling their cousins: "Hey, Slavka, guess what?" The way the Russians were about money made the Japanese look like Zen saints. "See what I mean?" I sighed. "I'm gonna do some overnight work here, just to catch up. Some of these buildings will have to go. Waterfront, lot of weather damage. She thinks it's gonna be like the old days, she's wrong."

"And what if the AI rejects her claim?"

I leaned toward the screen. "Then I pay a big fine, M. Richler."

"As long as you're aware," she said placidly, then contemplated me a moment. "I got a call from Suzanne Powell just now."

"Is that so?"

"Yes. She has an idea for reopening the island's recreation area. Do know anything about this?"

I slammed back in the seat. Suz... That bitch... Prancing back to Lola without even telling me. God forbid what was going to happen tomorrow morning...

"I see that you don't. Well, goodnight, M. Naylor." She hesitated, her shields flickering. "You mentioned working all night. How do you intend to do that?"

"Slap on a stim patch. Whaddaya think?"

"You have a medical certificate?"

"Aw, will you stop..."

She nodded and cut off. Good thing she hadn't pushed it. As a matter of fact, I hadn't been cleared.

As I sat back to reflect on my forthcoming remarks to Suz, there was loud barking from down the boardwalk. Dogs in their myriads appeared, old Sarah walking behind them.

"Hello," she said as she went past. I nodded and switched the comp to call up some data then thought of hitters.

She was fifty feet down, surrounded by romping mutts. I opened the door and called, "Hey, Sarah."

She went on with no sign that she'd heard. I remembered the hearing aid and went after her. Dogs ran joyously to greet me as I caught up.

"Sarah," I said, pulling at my ear. Her mouth made an 'o' and she turned the thing up.

"You know, it's dangerous to be out here at night."

"Oh no, there's no one else around."

"What about hitters?"

"No one would bother me. And if they did, my darlings would take care of them."

I looked down at her darlings, sitting on their haunches with tongues unfurled. Sarah patted my arm and walked on. "It's sweet of you."

I started to swing away, but the buildings suddenly looked like barracks for hitters. The hitter central command. Their main army group. I shrugged and turned back to her.

Sarah seemed delighted as I fell in step. "Oh, you're going to walk with me. That's so nice."

"Yeah. Good night for it. Walk the dogs."

We went on in silence for a few yards, then she raised her stick to point at what appeared to be a shed for storing corpses. "That was Stan's place," she said. "Salt water taffy. Did you ever have salt water taffy?"

"Don't think so."

She sighed. "You young people." Another flourish of the stick. "Peg's souvenirs..."

So I got the grand tour. Hot dogs, T-shirts, souvenirs, take your own picture, souvenirs, some kind of candy that was made out of cotton, souvenirs...

·  ·  ·

Then she dragged me off the boardwalk and things got interesting: the tunnel of love, a couple haunted houses (didn't look any different than what I'd been seeing for six months), a roller rink, a freak show (bearded lady, hermaphrodite—sounded like biosculpt to me), something where they got in cars and attacked each other.

And the Cyclone, Norman's first job. I stared up at it, teeth on edge, convinced the damn thing was going to come down right on top of us. "But what did they do with it?"

"Why, rode it, of course."

It came to me; I'd seen a clip of it once. People piling into little carts, then roaring up and down those curves at about sixty plus, this for amusement. I shook my head and turned away. A different breed.

I gestured at the tower in the near distance. "What did they do there? Hang themselves?"

"Oh, you're so funny. No, they used to be lifted up," she rose on her toes. "And then come down again. On parachutes."

Lifted up and parachuted down. Jesus Christ Almighty. Well, I suppose it was better than being machine-gunned by a crackhead.

We'd gone nearly full circle. The hover came into sight and I turned to her. "Did people really come here for all that?"

"Oh yes."

"Lots of 'em."

The stick rose to encompass the whole area. "This used to be filled with people. Every weekend; families, children, young couples. You could barely walk. And the lights, and the music.... Oh, I know about the other places, the Disney ones, but nothing was ever like Coney Island. Norman loved it so much. Just like a little boy..."

I tried to picture it: people battering their way through junkies and gangs for the privilege of being thrown off a tower. Probably had to pay for it, too.

Sarah was silent, clutching the top of her stick. Without turning she said, "You're not really going to tear it all down, are you?"

"Well, you know. It's like this. I mean hey. The AI..."

"Yes, the AI. Suzanne told me about that. It's some kind of computer, isn't it? Do you think a machine would understand?"

"Maybe. Yeah. Pretty good chance."

She patted my arm. "Let's hope so."

I watched her walk off, convoyed by her dogs, then hauled myself into the hover. I glanced at the foul buildings, the tower, the Cyclone.

There wasn't anything so rotten, so burnt-out, so beat-up that somebody didn't want to save it. No, that wasn't true. When we did the Bronx, did anyone come up and say, "Aw, my old grandad sold dope on that corner, can't we keep it?" Or Red Hook: "The Mob used to dump people off that dock, it's a historic site."

No. But now, right on the ass-end of the whole project, here it comes: Jeeze, Craig, she's an old lady. Aw, Craig, have a heart. M. Naylor, the AI will rule on this matter two minutes before deadline.

I'd asked my Dad once how people had been able to stand it back in the 20th; the crime, the corruption, the savagery in the streets. "Well, Craig," he'd told me. "People who live in shit up to their necks get used to the stink. Some of them even come to enjoy it."

I looked after Sarah. Fine case of that here. Well, she could have her house, the whole damn block if she wanted. People could come visit the Grand Custodian anytime they pleased. But if the AI said the rest had to go, it'd go. Even if I had to flatten the whole goddam island personally.

I grabbed the first-aid kit and slapped a patch on my arm, then called up the analysis data and got to work.

• • •

A noise awoke me, and it was a moment before I realized it was barking. I squinted through the windshield at the morning sun.

I'd worked until just before dawn then took an inhibitor to get at least a couple hours sleep. I felt played-out; not only the allnighter but the whole past few months piling up on me. I rubbed my forehead and was getting up for some coffee when I saw Suz walking toward her van.

Marching over I found the door open. I paused to put on a suitable gorilla face then leapt up, arms wide.

Suz looked at me as I tore my cap off and threw it on the floor. I shambled forward, knocking some printouts off a desk. Looming over her, I raised my fists to the sky. Conspiracy, I shouted. Betrayal. Going behind my back to Lola, the enemy. Turning on me, the whole pack of them—their boss who loved them, who paid overtime without complaint, who faithfully followed union regs, who gave them sick days without suspicion, who had trained them, valued them, nurtured them...

She waited quietly until I slammed the side of the van a final time. "You were on stim last night, weren't you?"

I glared and she turned back to the screen. "You better watch that. You'll get sick."

"What about this rebuilding crap?"

"It'd be nice to have a place like that. People get tired of virtuals. They're so boring, you know it's all phony."

"Nobody would come out here."

"Why not?"

"Because it's a rathole!"

"It isn't."

I waved at the door. "Goddamnit, go out and take a look..."

"I've seen it," she snapped, slamming shut the timebook. "You know, Craig, you've got a problem. There's a thing you have about this city. You can see it when we tear a block down. You get this look on your face, not just a job-well-done expression either, but like you really enjoy it..."

"Is this Suz Powell speaking? The woman who set the amps that blew down half of Brooklyn?"

"That's just it, dammit!" She sounded really angry. "All those houses, one after the other. It's depressing. You can't stop thinking about it..."

"Come off it. You know what went on around here. Riots, muggings, rapes. People couldn't walk the streets. Cops wore body armor and carried shotguns..."

Suz leapt up and stamped her foot. "And that's all of it, huh? Well, you're wrong, Mister Naylor. They had lives here. They loved each other. They had families. You make it sound like the Dark Ages. It wasn't like that."

"Fuckin'-A right it was."

With a sound of disgust she sank back into the seat. "You just don't care. I can't understand it. Were any of your folks ever mugged?"

"We didn't live around here."

"You must have heard some wild stories when you were a kid, Craig."

I snorted and turned to leave. At the door I paused. "How you gonna get the money for this?"

"Sell shares. How do you think?"

"I suppose you'll set up a crack house they can walk through."

"Oh, foof," she said, waving a hand at me.

The rest of the crew had drifted in. They eyed me sullenly: mean old Craig wants to knock poor Sarah's houses down. We'll fix his ass. They hadn't even saved me a donut.

I sent them off surveying while I started the real work. Alone, which is not smart: last week a new kid had gone through a floor up in Bensonhurst. Ribs and legs broken, fractured pelvis, concussion. He'd been hospitalized for two whole days. But I was in no mood for company.

I wanted things ready in case the AI's decision went against the old lady. I dragged along a case of amps with the analysis printouts in my pocket. Not that I'd need those; nothing special about these structures. They'd crack as soon as I hit the button, no problem—I could smell the mildew and damp rot as I went up the steps.

Taking my time, I eased down to the basement—a thrill-ride in itself—found the main load-bearing beams and looked them over. As I'd figured, they wouldn't need any treatment. With newer buildings you often had to inject some fungus and let them sit for a day or two, same as you do for brick structures, but that wasn't a factor here.

I took out an amp, noticing that the case had been opened, and stuck it on the beam. It's a bit of an art: they have to be planted differently every time for maximum effect. The amps were metal and plastic cones weighing about ten pounds, a bit bigger than my hand. The cores were small chunks of plastique tailored to give a nice rumble in the subsonic range which was then amplified by baffles and electronics. One of them could blow a hole in a concrete embankment. Two could bring down any building you pointed out.

I finished and went on to the next building. As I worked I thought about what Suz had said. Loved each other. Raised families ... and then ran out when things got tough. Not my problem; the government will handle it; the plague of the late 20th, everybody deciding to take a break for a decade or two and let things slide a little.

And slid they had: virtually every major city had been in the same shape as Brooklyn by the time they woke up. Some of them didn't even exist anymore: Detroit, Paterson, L. A. They'd gone the same place Brooklyn and Queens were going.

But what impressed Suz was a loony old hermit hanging around to please her husband's ghost.

I was wrapping up the fifth house when I heard something and flashed the light to see Patel at the top of the stairs, eagle eyes glittering.

"Watch it," I called out. I'd nearly fallen through coming in; the risers were about gone.

He worked his way down, jumping the last few feet. "Good news," he said as he hunkered down next to me. "Hitters on the way."

I grimaced. An unknown number of armed, crazed degenerates on the march. Good news.

"Cruiser spotted 'em couple miles west, walking the middle of the street bold as you please. Scattered before we could spank 'em, but they're comin'."

"They're comin'," I said.

"Yep. Now I was thinkin'." He raised a gleaming claw. "They want your hover. Well okay. Why not leave it out in the open and deck 'em when they come runnin'? What you think of that?"

"I don't."

He chuckled. "Didn't believe you would. So we'll do this instead. You hang around in the hover. We'll give you the word when they show up and you take off. Straight out over the water. Then we'll clean up."

"Are you kidding me?"

The eyes suddenly went ferocious. "Why no, Naylor, I'm not. I ain't a kiddin' man. Never was. Way it is, we don't flush 'em, then it's house to house. I don't like that. Takes time, and my boys can get hurt. We need bait, and your vehicle is it."

That's a half-million dollar hovercraft you're talking about, you hillbilly. Leave it sitting in a free-fire zone with me at the wheel. Get your own vehicle.

"...now I don't want to go this route, Naylor, but I'll invoke police powers I have to."

I tapped the flash on my knee. His shadow capered on the wall behind him. "Shit," I said.

He reached over and clapped my shoulder. "That's the spirit. I like a man with spunk."

"Now don't you worry none," he said as he got up. "This place will be sewed up tight. Drop flares soon's they poke their noses out. Bright as day. You'll see."

He clambered up the stairs. "Chief," I called. "How'd you know I was down here?"

"Your crew." A sort of concerned osprey look appeared. "Something eatin' on them, too. One of 'em called you Nero. I'd look into that. Word to the wise."

He vanished and I reached for an amp. "Spunk," I said as I slapped it on the beam. "Nero."

•  •  •

The Narrows arcology glowed against the last streak of dusk. That and the Sharpton Tower were the only signs of life; the darkness could have hid the Gobi or Hell.

I sat behind the wheel, eyes darting from shadow to shadow. The radio was on the police freak, the cops perping and situationing each other. I hoped they'd speak English when they gave me the word.

The crew was long gone, all except Suz. When I'd asked her to warn the old lady she'd decided to stay overnight.

"Naylor, you there?"

I grabbed the mike. "Yeah."

"Speak up, dammit. Been calling you the past minute." Patel's voice went into a bland official tone. "Observed suspects proceeding across causeway yours. You got that?"

"Uh-huh."

"Well, sit tight."

I looked out the side window, opened the door to peer over the top, fiddled with the mirrors. I listened for a moment but heard nothing. There hadn't been any cruisers around all night but that was probably standard cop procedure.

Patel had told me to leave the turbines off, an idea that did not charm me. It took only twenty seconds to get them rolling but that could be twenty seconds too many. I grabbed the key and concentrated on the radio chatter but then jumped as I saw a shape running toward me down the boardwalk.

That bastard, I thought. Y'all don't worry none, Naylor. We'll take keer them crackers, you jes sit tight, heh-heh.

The turbines roared behind me. My sweaty hands fumbled on the board as I hit what absolutely had to be the fan switch.

I was turning the wheel when the cleaning system started spraying the windshield.

Cursing, I shut it off and was about to switch on the fans when the dark figure, slightly distorted by cleaner, yelled: "Craig!"

I opened the door as Suz ran up. "Sarah's gone,"she said breathlessly. "She slipped out. She thinks you're going to blow the buildings tonight."

"Where'd she go?"

"I don't know."

I waved at the dark houses. "How the hell am I supposed to find her in there? The hitters are coming!"

Suz raised clenched fists and shook them. "Ohh... I'm so stupid," she said, then turned and ran back the way she'd come.

Staring after her, I muttered to myself a while then jumped out and headed for the row I'd set up earlier, thinking that one of the loathsome swine I honored by calling my crew might have dropped her the word. Behind me the hover turbines rumbled but I ignored them.

I was about to climb the steps when my foot hit something compact and heavy. Grasping it, I smiled for the first time that day: it was an amp. The other was probably out here too. I ran down the rest of the row, seeing amps in front of each. There were howls rising in the distance, along with occasional gunshots.

At the sixth house I found her. She stood blinking in the flashlight beam, arms full of amps. "Young man," she said as I came up the stairs. "I trusted you. You said you'd wait for the machine to tell you what to do."

"Lady..."

She held the amps out to me. "And look what I find. All I asked for was a little time..."

I was about to start yelling but I remembered the hearing aid and lunged at her instead, picking her up and throwing her over my shoulder. As I ran for the boardwalk I heard more howls, voices yelling, "Tammany!" over and over.

A chill went through me. Patel had kept that to himself. This wasn't any ordinary hitter gang. It was Tammany Hall, the oldest, toughest, most brutal of them all.

I wasn't halfway to the hover when a figure ran onto the boardwalk and yodelled at me. Swerving away, I spotted an old shack and set Sarah down next to it.

I turned back to see the hitter twenty yards away and closing fast. He was wearing a loincloth, leather vest and tricorn hat. His face and chest were painted and eight-inch-long dinosaur horns protruded above his eyes. He was carrying a rifle tipped with a bayonet. No stunners for this bunch.

"Young man," Sarah said sternly. I waved her back but then felt her hand on my arm.

"Goddamit." I swung toward her just as she caught sight of the hitter. Her eyes went wide and she raised a hand to her mouth. I noticed she was still holding an amp and grabbed it from her.

I moved slowly toward the hitter, switching the amp to manual. He howled and aimed the bayonet at me. Answering yodels came, way too close. As he poised to leap I armed the amp and tossed it at him.

He backed off as it landed at his feet, not knowing what it was. I counted to five, and then again. The amp just sat there.They'd screwed me: my own crew. Defused the fuckers while I wasn't looking.

Footsteps and shouts came from around the corner, suddenly drowned out by cruiser engines. On top of it all I could have sworn I heard barking.

The hitter inched forward, nudging the amp with a filthy toe. Raising the bayonet high, he gave me a nasty laugh. He lowered his head, the points of those horns seeming to be lined up right on my belly. Glaring madly, he yelled, "Tammany!" just as the rest of them raced onto the boardwalk, six cruisers roared over the rooftops and flares burst into brilliance.

The hitter stopped, catching sight of something behind me. I glanced back to see Sarah's dogs raging into view. They must have been barking their heads off but I couldn't hear a thing.

I leapt for the hitter and brought him down. We landed on the old wood just as the dogs reached us.

I got loose and rolled away; they weren't interested in me. Sarah ran out, calling, but the dogs paid no attention. Getting to my feet I hustled her behind the shed again as a cruiser roared ten feet overhead.

A stunner thumped; dogs and hitter collapsed. Beyond them the rest of Tammany—there must have been fifty of them—were busy doing the same.

Then I saw that a pair had reached the hover and were climbing aboard, waving their guns in triumph. I started running but hadn't got ten feet before the skirts puffed out, blowing trash across the boardwalk.

Within seconds it was fifty yards down and picking up speed. I pushed on, not closing the distance any. A cruiser appeared, dropping to within five feet of the hover, and a cop leaned out to fire a stunner right into the cockpit.

I came to a halt as the hover started to drift. I held my breath, following its course as it swayed across the boardwalk, nodding to myself when I saw where it was headed and closing my eyes as a two-year old Nakamura Duster with twenty payments left on it smashed into Stan's Salt Water Taffy.

I turned away. One of the flares had landed on a rooftop and the house was ablaze, burning as only a hundred-year old structure could. It was one that I'd set up that afternoon. All that work and now look.

I felt the blast of a cruiser and a PA blared at me. "Naylor, you get your rump under cover, hear?"

Waving vaguely, I walked on. As I passed the hitter he rolled on his side and pointed his horns at me. "I want an attorney," he croaked.

"You go to hell," I told him.

Sarah came out from behind the shed. She looked at her dogs, at the blazing house, at the big gap the Duster had made, at me. She was raising her hands to her face when she collapsed.

I got to her a second after Suz did.

. . .

"Somebody see to these dawgs," Patel was yelling.

I leaned against Suz's van. The rest of the night had been a bedlam of sirens, flames, fire engines and paddy wagons—not to mention the ambulance for Sarah. They'd managed to save most of the island, including the amusement park, not including my hover. Wisps of smoke were still rising from the foam. I turned to gaze out over the sea. Nice morning, anyway.

"Who's lookin' after these dawgs?"

The van door opened and Suz leapt out. She inspected me aloofly for a second. "Lola,"she said.

"Goddamnit..." Patel shouted. I bobbed my head. "Dawgs,"I said. Suz sniffed and strolled off.

The most unpopular man on Coney Island climbed wearily into the van. The crew had shown up for work, thanks to me being too much of an idiot to call the hotel. They'd stood around shaking their heads at the ruins, knowing Naylor's vicious handiwork when they saw it. I'd sent them back. "With pay," Terri had said, not a question. I agreed, too tired to bring up amp sabotage. They'd all left except for Suz and Spags.

Lola nodded and started rattling away: police error, not my fault, so the AI had spoken. It wanted a report, though, soon as possible, like today.

"...and, you'll be pleased to hear, the title ruling has come down. The island is now provisionally owned by Sarah Halder and Nero Development, N.A., subject to other claims." She smiled, a unique event. "So it's turned out fine after all."

I couldn't bear it. "No thanks to you, Counselor."

Her shields dropped and I saw her eyes clearly, wide and hurt. She lowered her head. "Who do you think argued this case, anyway?"

I slumped in the seat. "Lola, I'm..."

Blanker than ever, the shields bored into me. "The Brighton Beach titles have been cleared," she said in a throaty voice. "You can get busy there now."She hit her board and the data came through.

"Hey, Lola..."

She touched her temple and the shields vanished completely. "The name is M. Richler, asshole."

The screen darkened and the master of tact got up and stumbled out.

Patel was waiting, brisk with victory. I noticed the eyes didn't seem bloodshot.

"Just got the final report," he said. "Bagged 'em all. Last ones just an hour ago."

"Uh."

"Only one fatality—he's gettin' revived right now. Was down for over five, though. He'll be stupid a month or two."

"Hmm."

A claw lifted. "Thinkin' of puttin' you in for a citation."

"For what, losing my Duster?"

He laughed and looked around him. "So. Busted Tammany. Feels damn good." He shook his head at the wreckage then eyed me slyly. "Fucked it up otherwise, though."

"We sure did."

"Well, do right next time." Winking at me, he turned and walked off.

I went on myself, past the toasted souvenir stands, tattoo parlors, hovercraft, to a spot where the boardwalk fence still stood. I climbed atop it, feeling it sway beneath me.

A perfect day, sky blue, soft salt breeze, warm with the promise of more heat coming. I recalled that it was Friday. Back when the years had ones in front of them they'd have been on their way, families, couples, old folks, to jump off towers, get tattooed and eat salt water taffy.

Sure they would. I looked it over, the shabby, sea-tortured remnants. For the life of me I couldn't picture it any different than it was now. I felt a touch of sadness at that, the realization that I was a man of my time, that there were some things I would simply never grasp.

Spags appeared, sneaking from between two buildings. He was carrying a big rectangular something on top of his head and as he turned I saw it was a sign reading "Nathan's."

I smiled at the Cyclone, looming high and immortal in the morning sky. But maybe they were right. If old New York had to have a monument, it might as well be Coney Island.

I slid off the fence and started out after Spags. That damn sign didn't belong to him, and I was sure that Sarah would miss it.